A SUMMER OF DREAMS

Tanya Jean Russell

SAPERE
BOOKS

A SUMMER OF DREAMS

Published by Sapere Books.

20 Windermere Drive, Leeds, England, LS17 7UZ,
United Kingdom

saperebooks.com

ISBN: 978-1-80055-289-0

CHAPTER ONE

Her foot catching on the cracked paving slab that had been on the 'things she'd repair once she had some spare money' list since forever, Susie Lucas snorted. Thankfully, her lifelong addiction to trainers meant she didn't have to worry about tripping over in heels on top of the hazard that was the footpath from the home she still shared with her mother Dorothy.

One day she might get to live in a place of her own, instead of being stuck paying off the second mortgage she'd had to take out to repay her dad's theft, but surrounded by reminders of just how much she still had to pay for, it was hard to believe it could ever happen. The fact that the first mortgage was almost finished wasn't going to help anywhere near enough. Giving her mum a smile, Susie turned her thoughts away from dreams of a future that would never happen.

The walk to the Parker family home was less than fifteen minutes, but her mum was out of breath by the time they were knocking on the large front door. She knew Dorothy would have been much happier if Susie had just driven them both the short distance, but making her mum walk whenever she could was the only way Susie could think of to try to improve her fitness. Despite the fact she was at least half a dozen dress sizes bigger than she had been when her husband had left her, Dorothy seemed to draw further and further into herself. Hopefully, getting her to come to Evie Parker's ninth birthday party would help. If nothing else, Susie knew Grace Parker — Evie's grandmother — and her mother-in-law Agnes would make Dorothy feel welcome and look after her. Plus, Susie had a feeling that she would be wanting a drink to get through the afternoon. The older generation of Honeyford were fine, but her own generation never let her forget she was a Lucas.

"Susie, you're early. Come on in," Maggie said, balancing a large jug in one hand as she swung the door open with the other. Maggie was the fiancée of Nathan Parker — the middle of the five Parker brothers — and one of Susie's oldest friends.

"I thought we'd get here early enough to help set up," Susie said.

"Ah, that's thoughtful. We're all set, but Sarah and Paul are about to let Evie open her presents from the family if you want to join us? We're all out in the back garden."

"That would be great," Susie said, steering her mum through the house.

"Dorothy, come and sit here," Agnes called, gesturing to a high-backed cushioned chair between her and Grace.

Dorothy smiled and headed over, sinking into the chair with a barely supressed sigh of relief at sitting down. Susie kept a smile on her face but scanned the assembled group, waiting for any sign of judgement. Realising that there wouldn't be any, she sank onto the ground next to Maggie, the array of blankets making the place look like a floral commune. Susie smiled at the assembled Parkers and their respective partners; they had always been kind to her, but since Maggie had arrived back in the village, they had really made her feel a part of the family.

"Here, you look like you could do with one of these." Tess — the local baker — eased herself down as she passed Susie a drink.

"Definitely," Susie said, accepting the glass of white wine with an outstretched hand. "Just how many cakes have you been roped into baking for this one?"

"Enough," Tess said with a smile. "At least Sarah and Paul always insist on paying, unlike some of the other parents around here, who seem to think the fact our kids go to school together means I should be bringing the cakes to their birthday parties as a gift."

"Ah, the joys of parenthood," Susie said, knowing that Tess's son Finn was in the same class as Evie, which meant he'd be on the same circuit of endless kids' parties as today's birthday girl seemed to be on.

"Well, they shouldn't be encouraging the children to eat such sugary food anyway," said Kate, the girlfriend of Joe, the youngest Parker brother. Kate had been dating Joe for nearly two years, which was eighteen months longer than anyone had expected for the lad who had the attention span of a toddler when it came to anything important in life.

"It's nice to have a treat at a party, though," Susie said, wanting to head off the inevitable row between the health-obsessed Kate and Tess, whose bakery was renowned for the sort of treats that were at complete odds with Kate's view of the world.

"It's when it's more than an occasional treat that it's an issue," Kate said, standing and heading towards Joe.

Pleased that the debate couldn't escalate, Susie closed her eyes behind her sunglasses and let the relaxed atmosphere wash over her. The warmth of the sunshine seemed to seep through to her bones, and the chatter of the gathered Parkers hummed around her until she felt the last of her tension ease away.

It was only as the sound of a deep voice reached her that she realised Dean was here.

Her shoulders immediately stiffened. At a time when everyone had wanted to ram it down her throat at every opportunity, he had made her feel like she didn't have to be defined by the fact she was a Lucas. He hadn't made her forget; he had made her believe it didn't matter. Right up until the moment it did.

Susie forced herself to look up as he walked over to join them, determined to remain unbroken, unaffected. Her smile hurt as she watched him. She would meet his gaze with confidence if he actually looked her way, but she'd realised over the last couple of years that Dean went out of his way not to. The few times he had glanced at her, the skin around his pale blue eyes seemed to tighten. She was never sure what was worse, the times he didn't look at her, or the times he did. Thankfully, they didn't see much of each other these days. That's what happened when your supposed best friend just upped and left you to move to London.

Watching Evie's face light up at the sight of her uncle, Susie took a big gulp of her drink, feeling grateful she hadn't driven. She was going to need more than one drink to get through a kids' party with Dean. He'd been her best friend for six years before he'd moved away. He hadn't lived in Honeyford for seven years. She needed to move on; they both did. She needed to find a way to deal with him that didn't squeeze her heart every time he came home. They needed to find a way back to some sort of friendship, but she was damned if she could figure out how the hell to achieve that when Dean still went out of his way to avoid being in the same space as her.

CHAPTER TWO

"I'm so glad you made it. You won't believe how much Oliver has grown since you were last here," Grace Parker said to her son as he leant in to kiss her cheek.

Dean smiled at his mum and did his best not to listen to yet another example of how amazing his parents thought his brothers were. His second eldest brother Chris, and Chris's wide Paula's son Oliver was nearly five months old, and while Dean completely agreed with Grace's assessment of how adorable her second grandchild was, to Dean it just felt like another way in which he was falling short in life.

He'd already had it from his dad on the trip from the station. Much as he loved his parents, he would have been much happier getting a taxi. At least that way he would have been spared the endless list of things that his siblings had done to make his parents proud since his last visit. Even as an adult, being the middle child sucked.

"Did you hear me?" Grace asked, breaking into Dean's thoughts.

"Yes, it's great," Dean said, having no clue what Grace had been talking about, but knowing he was fairly safe saying something positive. Shaking off the gloom that seemed to descend every time he came home, he forced a smile and moved around, making sure to sit a little further away from his mum and easing himself into a space on the blankets that fanned across the top corner of his parents' lawn. At least if he could sit next to his Granny Agnes, he'd be distracted from the other thing he liked to avoid when he came home — well, person, not thing.

Dean realised his mistake as soon as his backside hit the ground. In his efforts not to sit next to Grace, he found himself almost opposite Susie. She was directly in his eyeline. He swallowed hard, trying to focus on Evie, who sat in the middle of the distorted circle of her family, waiting for her presents. He couldn't look at Susie, because if he spent more than a few seconds looking at her, he stopped seeing the beautiful, cropped hair that made her look like a mischievous pixie. He stopped seeing the dark eyes that swallowed the top of her face and made men stop in their tracks. All he could see was the blood trickling down her forehead, and the olive skin faded to an almost translucent white. He wouldn't see the slim, lithe figure that had tortured him during his teenage years. Instead, he would see her being cut from his car, her thigh crushed. He'd see everything he had done wrong. No, better to look at something else, anything else.

He smiled at his Granny Agnes as she bent over the side of her lounger and patted his shoulder.

"I saved you the best one," she said, holding out a napkin parcel.

"I hope you don't expect me to eat whatever that is?" Dean asked, a smile stretching across his face. Her bizarre concoctions were legendary, and as far as he knew, he was the only one who dared to tease her about them. Well, he was the only one who got away with it.

"You know full well you'll eat it and love it," Agnes said, her answering smile a match for his own. "Come here and give me a hug."

He got up onto his knees and wrapped his arms around her. "Well, it feels like you haven't been eating any of your own creations," he said, holding Agnes close and trying not to let the fact she felt thinner than ever worry him.

"You hush, you know better than to comment on a woman's figure," she said. "You're not too old for me to smack your bottom."

"Sorry, ma'am," he said, smiling at the image of her attempting to follow through on her threat. "Are you okay, though?" Dean pulled back and studied her face. The skin that had been crinkly for as long as he could remember was developing a crêpe-thin appearance, giving the formidable woman an air of frailty that made him worry for her.

"Don't fuss, I'm absolutely fine. How are you?" she asked.

"I'm good," he said, opening the parcel. The pasty looked delicious, but he knew from experience that looks could be deceptive. He took a bite. As the flavours began to come through, Dean decided that listening to his mother tell him how wonderful his brothers were might have been preferable. "What is this?" he managed to garble, desperately trying to chew enough to swallow. He wasn't perfect, but even he knew better than to spit out his granny's baking.

"It's mini pain au chocolat with anchovy."

"Okay," he said carefully. "Interesting choice."

"I know, I'm being cosmopolitan. I thought it would impress Patrick at the club."

"Who's Patrick?"

"Just a friend. He's new to the area, and I don't want him thinking we're all backwards just because he's from Bristol."

Dean smiled at Agnes thinking Bristol was another world when it was less than an hour away. "I've missed you," he said, giving her arm a gentle squeeze. She was the only family member who had never seemed to care that he wasn't perfect, who hadn't spent his entire youth telling him how to be better.

"You got the train home again?" Agnes asked, ignoring his statement.

Dean froze; it might have seemed a straightforward question, but he knew better. "Yes," he said, when he could force the word out. "It's much quicker, and I can get work done while I'm travelling." It was his stock response, and no one else in the family ever questioned him on it.

"It's been seven years," Agnes said, her small hand patting his cheek as she spoke. "It's time."

Dean shook his head, not knowing what to say, only knowing he wanted the conversation to stop.

"Alright, Dean?" Joe said, taking a spot on the blanket next to him. "Don't tell me Granny has persuaded you to eat her baking already?"

Dean turned to look at his youngest brother, grateful for the interruption even if it came from the darling of the family. "You should try one. These are really good," he said, a smirk curling his lips as he met Joe's horrified gaze.

"Oh, I'd love to, but we want to make sure there are enough for the guests when they come, don't we?" Joe said, tripping over the words.

"Don't you worry about that. I made more than enough for everyone," Agnes said.

A little warmth spread through Dean's chest at the realisation Agnes had only saved one for him; even if it was disgusting, the thought was what mattered.

Spending his weekend at a nine-year-old's birthday party definitely wasn't what his London friends and colleagues would expect him to be doing, but as he watched Evie rip through the wrapping on her gifts he accepted that — even as he tried to avoid seeing Susie — he loved being here, surrounded by his family. He knew he wasn't the favourite son, and he certainly wasn't anyone's favourite brother, but he loved this bunch of people. Unconsciously, his gaze flicked to Susie, who was fidgeting as she passed a gift to Evie.

"Art lessons?" Evie asked as she pulled the wrapping off.

Waving a tin of what Dean assumed were paints around, Evie leapt to her feet and flung her arms around Susie.

"We'll get to hang out, and you can help me paint amazing pictures like you do," Evie said.

Susie flushed, as though relieved that Evie liked the gift. "Almost," she said. "We'll hang out together and I can help you paint amazing pictures that only you can create."

Evie spun around at a speed that Dean was sure would leave her ridiculously dizzy. "Can we start now?" she asked.

"Perhaps we should have your party first," Susie said with a laugh.

"Why don't you open your present from Uncle Dean?" Sarah said, steering her hyperactive daughter towards him.

"Here you go, pumpkin," Dean said, awkwardly handing over the rectangular box.

Watching as Evie opened the box containing the Raspberry Pi and set of accessories, he realised that it maybe wasn't the best gift for a nine-year-old, but when he'd asked around at the office, he'd been assured it was the perfect gift for getting a child started in programming, and the thought of getting one of his family interested in something he felt so passionately about had been too hard to resist. The warmth of the day seemed to intensify, and his cheeks burned.

Easing onto his knees, he leant towards Evie, determined to try to salvage his poor choice.

"This bit here goes into your computer," he explained. "And I can show you how to build a robot." He smiled at Evie, doing his best to ignore the sinking sensation in his stomach as she frowned down at the collection of components. He should have bought her something different. He should have asked Sarah or his eldest brother Paul what Evie wanted.

Evie looked back up at him, her features brightening. "We can do it together?" she asked, her voice lilting with hope. This kid was going to kill him, she was so adorable.

"Definitely," he said, wondering when he would find time to visit often enough to build a robot with his niece. Oh well, if it kept her smiling at him like that, he'd figure something out. If nothing else, he could video chat her through it.

Evie's school friends and their respective parents had begun arriving as soon as Evie had finished unwrapping her presents, and Dean found himself surrounded by people he remembered from his own school days.

"Yeah, I'm working up in Bristol now, doing sales for a building firm," Stephen said. Dean vaguely remembered being a couple of years behind him at school.

"What kind of building work?"

"Just new housing estates. You know, the sort of thing where every house looks identical," Stephen replied with a shrug, before gesturing to a couple of much younger kids with chocolate-smeared faces as they toddled along, trying to keep up with the bigger kids. "It's not exciting, but its steady work, which matters with my two monsters to support."

Dean smiled at Stephen and took another swig of his beer. He didn't understand his awkwardness about his job. Most people didn't get to do the sort of job that really made them happy. "Looking after your family is the best thing you can do," Dean said. "It must be great to be working locally enough to get home to them every day."

Stephen smiled back, his shoulders easing a fraction. "Yes, it is." He looked across the garden at his wife, sharing a private smile with her. "That's Laura."

Dean realised she didn't look at all familiar. "Where did you two meet?" he asked.

"She was here on holiday with her friends — some sort of hen weekend thing at the old Miller place. You know the one that was converted into an Airbnb place with a hot tub and everything?" At Dean's nod, Stephen continued, "We met in the Angel Arms. We hit it off and kept in touch when she went home."

The Angel Arms was the only pub that had been close enough for them to drink in without needing either a designated driver or a small fortune and at least three weeks' notice to book a taxi when they'd all grown up here, and it hadn't changed since, so Dean could well imagine it was benefiting from the Millers' place being turned into holiday accommodation.

"You'd better not be telling him that we slept together that weekend," Laura said as she joined them, handing her husband a bottle of beer.

"As if I'd share all our secrets," Stephen said, raising his eyebrows at her.

Dean laughed as she gave her husband a good-natured shove before slipping her arm around his waist and turning to watch the other guests. "I didn't realise it was Susie Lucas's dad who stole all that PFTA money," Laura said, watching Susie walk towards her mother.

Dean froze. He couldn't believe people were still talking about it.

"She's been working at the school," Laura added, her tone thoughtful, as though questioning the wisdom of that bit of information.

"So?" Dean asked, his eyes focused on Susie, who was oblivious to the fact she was being talked about.

"Oh, well, you know," Laura said, stumbling over her words.

"No, I don't," Dean said. "What are you suggesting?"

Laura flinched, and Dean realised his tone had been a lot sharper than he'd intended, but for Christ's sake, were people really still bringing this up? Couldn't they just let Susie be? He frowned at Laura but didn't bother trying to smooth things over with her, and when she and Stephen eased away from him, he let them go.

Moving to the wall, he leant back, just perching on the brick as he watched the people gathered. How had he missed it? Everywhere he looked, familiar faces were glancing furtively at Susie and her mother. He frowned, his jaw tightening. How much of that was because of his own part in damaging Susie's reputation?

"You look ready to take on an army," Nathan said, perching next to him.

Dean turned to his younger brother and shook his head to clear his building frustration. "I'm fine, just bored of small talk," he said.

Nathan studied him for a moment, as though debating whether to push. Obviously deciding to leave it, he clinked his bottle against Dean's. "Forgiven me for punching you yet?" Nathan asked with raised eyebrows.

Dean had all but forgotten about that. He was more likely to hold a grudge against his brother for stealing his best friend away from him. After all, he'd barely seen Maggie since she'd moved back to Honeyford to live with Nathan.

"Forgiven me for letting you believe I was dating Maggie?" Dean asked, knowing that reminding Nathan of that was the quickest way to rile him.

"No," grumbled Nathan, the smile falling from his lips. "Just the idea makes me want to punch you again."

Dean laughed and raised his palms. "Chill out, little brother," he said. "She's made her choice. That rock on her finger makes that very clear."

"Just you remember it," Nathan said, the words almost a growl.

Dean laughed harder.

"Just as well I know you're useless at relationships, otherwise it'd be even harder to deal with your little subterfuge," Nathan said, taking a swig of his beer and reaching out to tug on Evie's ponytail as she ran up to them.

Dean froze; he might know he wasn't any good at relationships, but he definitely didn't like the fact being added to the 'list of things Dean isn't as good at as his brothers'. He scowled, trying to figure out how to respond so that Nathan wouldn't pick up on the sore spot. The last thing he needed was to give his siblings more ammunition.

"Will you help us with the catapults, Uncle Nathan?" Evie asked, running up to them, her previously spotless pink dress now soaking from the slip 'n' slide and sporting an array of grass stains.

"He'd love to," Dean said, giving Nathan a smile. They all adored Evie, but dealing with a dozen of her raucous classmates at the same time was a bit much for any of them.

"Thanks," Nathan said, rolling his eyes good-naturedly before putting his bottle down and letting Evie drag him away.

"See, totally whipped by women," Dean said, relieved to be spared from finishing the conversation with Nathan.

"Don't think it won't happen to you too, brother," Nathan said, looking back over his shoulder with a raised brow. "And I'm going to laugh myself stupid when it does."

CHAPTER THREE

"You're training to be a teacher, aren't you?" Jennifer asked, not a single hair slipping from her immaculate twist despite the gentle breeze that was floating through the garden. She took a delicate sip from her glass, her eyes fixed on Susie in expectation.

Susie decided to ignore the slight edge to Jennifer's voice as she asked the question. "Well, not yet, but as soon as I finish my degree, I'm hoping to start my teacher training," she said, focusing on keeping her shoulders relaxed as she carried on picking up the paper plates that were strewn across the blankets, and tossing them into a giant black bin liner.

"Oh. Do you think, well…" Jennifer began, glancing around at a couple of the other mums gathered. Almost all of the women had gone to the village primary school, so Susie knew them. "It's just that, do you think they will let you teach in a school?"

"Why wouldn't they?" Susie asked, fighting to keep her tone neutral. She met Jennifer's gaze and held it. Susie knew exactly what she was getting at, but she wasn't about to let her off the hook with half-formed innuendos and insults. If Jennifer wanted to make a point, she should damn well make it.

"Well, you know," Jennifer said, giving a nervous laugh, her gaze moving more furtively between her friends, the women who had obviously encouraged Jennifer to raise this topic.

"No?" Susie said, despite the fact she knew what Jennifer was saying.

Don't react, don't get angry, don't let them win. The mantra ran through her mind. She'd been thinking the same thing for fourteen years, exactly half of her life. *Don't react. As soon as you react, they win, they get to believe that everything they say about you is true.*

"Oh, well, never mind. I need to go to the bathroom," Jennifer said, the words tumbling out in her haste to extricate herself from the conversation she'd started.

Susie made herself stay and make small talk with the remaining women. It didn't matter that they got their entertainment by rehashing her family history. Her mum was never going to leave the village, which meant Susie was never going to leave. She had to get on with people, had to prove them wrong. Surely if she kept at it long enough, they'd form their own opinions about her. Eventually.

Catching the look of dismay on her mum's face, Susie realised she'd picked up on what had happened.

"Did you know my Susie has a placement with Sam Harrison?" Dorothy's voice cut through all conversation.

Susie cringed. While she applauded her mum's efforts to show people she could achieve something other than being Stanley Lucas's daughter — and the fact it was a flash of her old mum, the mum who'd stood up for herself and was a big part of the local community — she wished Dorothy hadn't decided to share something that wasn't going to happen.

For a moment, Susie let herself enjoy the flash of surprise that crossed the women's faces as the name registered. There were very few people who didn't know who Sam Harrison was. Aside from the fact most people couldn't have named another contemporary artist, Sam Harrison was also the very attractive host of a primetime TV show for budding artists, meaning he was a household name.

"That's amazing," Maggie said, crossing the garden and pulling Susie into a hug.

Quickly joined by Tess, they were soon swamped by people asking questions and expressing their congratulations.

CHAPTER FOUR

Standing in the hallway, Dean tried to resist the urge to walk in and smack whoever was talking. The party was due to finish in less than an hour, and it couldn't come soon enough for him.

"You know it won't be true, though, don't you?" a woman's voice said.

"I know, it's sad really. Poor Dorothy, resorting to lies about Susie's success. Everyone knows the family are liars and thieves. It was only a matter of time before something happened again."

"I suppose it's better it's something like a made-up opportunity, rather than something that hurts the community." The voice paused, before adding in a hushed tone, "Or worse."

"I know. It's just sad, though, because it's only a matter of time before it becomes obvious Susie doesn't have a placement, so why lie about it?"

"Well, that's the Lucas family for you."

Dean felt his fists clench; he'd been responsible for the 'worse' they were discussing as though it was entertainment, yet they seemed to be blaming Susie. All these years later and he was still hurting her.

"What's the Lucas family?" Susie's voice floated out to him, a saccharine quality to it that made it abundantly clear she'd heard at least as much as he had.

"Oh, nothing," the suddenly flustered woman said. "We were just grabbing these plates of sandwiches."

Two women appeared, hands full of dishes, and Dean glared at them as they dashed back into the garden.

After letting his glare follow them all the way out, he turned back and stepped into the kitchen. "You shouldn't listen to them," he said to Susie's back.

She was facing the wall, gripping the sides of the cupboards so hard her knuckles were white. "Brilliant, just brilliant," she muttered, her head rolling back so she stared at the ceiling. "Of course, *you* had to hear all of that too."

"They're small people with small lives. Ignore them."

"Thanks," she said, turning to face him. "Thanks for explaining to me how to deal with people I've been dealing with for the last fourteen years, and on my own for the last seven of those years. How did I cope before that insightful bit of advice?"

"I'm sorry," Dean said, looking at the floor, unable to hold her gaze as his stomach sank at the realisation that when he'd left, he hadn't taken the problems with him, he'd just left them to fall on her. "I'm sorry," he said again, looking up and meeting her dark eyes, wanting her to see his sincerity.

"It doesn't matter," Susie said. "They are going to be proved right. They'll have 'that time Dorothy made up a placement for Susie' to add to the Lucas family stories now, so I might as well get used to it."

"What do you mean?" Dean asked. "Isn't the placement real?"

Susie laughed, the sound brittle, as Maggie and Nathan walked in, carrying dirty plates and a black bin liner that was bursting at the seams. "It's real alright, but I won't be going."

"Why not?" Dean asked.

"What do you mean you won't be going?" Maggie asked, seconding Dean's question. "You can't pass up an opportunity like that. I mean, even I've heard of Sam Harrison. You nearly had a heart attack when you found out he was visiting the university."

"It's in London," Susie said, as though that explained everything.

Dean stared at her, wondering what he was missing. Maggie and Nathan were as clueless as he was.

"London, you know, as in the most expensive place in the country, a place too far away to commute to," Susie said, finding a bottle of wine and filling her glass before taking a massive gulp.

"So, stay in London," Dean said with a frown.

The lilt of children's laughter drifted into the kitchen, breaking through the tension that had been building. Susie's head turned to the window and she smiled at the sight of half a dozen of the partygoers racing across the front garden, soaked through and squealing. "I wish we were that age again. Life was much simpler," she said with a smile.

"We weren't even friends when we were that age," Dean said, his eyes on her, seeing the way her face seemed to soften as she watched the children play. "I much preferred the later years when we were."

Susie turned to meet his eyes, her smile real in a way he hadn't seen from her in years, and he knew that for just that instant, instead of only seeing the way things ended, they were connected to the friendship they had lost.

"Well, wishes don't make dreams come true," she said.

The words seemed to vibrate through him. She'd said them often enough when they were younger that, despite not having heard them for years, they seemed to awaken something in him. It was a phrase she and Dorothy had used a lot; it had almost been a mantra, a way of reminding themselves that they'd have to keep working to get back the life they wanted.

The four of them drifted back to the garden, and while Dean didn't want to let the subject of Susie's placement go, he knew that she didn't want to keep talking about it.

Watching Evie and her classmates playing on the slip 'n' slide Paul had set up in the back garden, Dean turned to Maggie and slung his arm around her shoulders.

"So, is my annoying little brother taking good care of you?" he asked, laughing as Nathan growled at him.

"You should know I don't need looking after," Maggie said, but she wrapped her arm around his waist as she said it, making it clear she hadn't taken offence.

He hadn't realised how much he'd missed hanging out with Maggie since she'd left London to move back home, but it was obvious just how happy she was.

Maggie chattered away about the next project she and Nathan planned to complete as part of the renovation of the barn they lived in together, and Dean let himself relax into the moment with his friends. He let himself enjoy the fact that, for once, he had been able to talk to Susie without his thoughts being consumed with the accident.

"How have those locusts masquerading as small humans eaten so much?" Susie asked as they watched more empty platters being carried into the kitchen.

Dean smiled at the description, his arm slipping from Maggie's waist.

"No idea," Nathan said. "But don't think you're off the hook so easily. There must be a way we can help you so you can take up the placement offer."

Susie didn't move, but it was as though every cell in her body had tensed at Nathan's casual statement. "I can't," she said.

"But you want to," Nathan persisted.

Susie sighed. "Of course I do. I'd have to be a moron not to want to go, but you know I can't," she said, her words pitched low, as though hoping to keep them just for Nathan.

Something inside of Dean stirred, frustrated that Nathan was the one being confided in, not him. He knew he'd lost that right years ago, but it felt wrong.

"You know we'd keep an eye on Dorothy for you," Nathan said.

Dean found his gaze seeking out Susie's mum. Finally finding Dorothy sitting in one of the green plastic chairs that only came out for parties, he frowned. She'd put some weight on over the last few years, a lot of weight, but lots of people did. Why did she need looking out for? Was she ill? What was wrong with her? Susie would be heartbroken if anything happened to her mum.

"Are we boring you?" Maggie asked, smacking Dean's arm and dragging him back to the conversation.

"What? Yes, of course," Dean said, making himself look as confused as he could, before winking at her. "What were you talking about?"

Maggie gave him an assessing look, and he realised she probably hadn't bought his attempt at casual; fortunately, she was the only person here who'd notice when he was using what she'd long since termed his 'don't give a damn attitude' for effect.

"You know I can't risk leaving my jobs either," Susie said, drawing Dean's attention back to her, but he didn't miss the amused look Maggie gave him. "I couldn't let people down like that."

"I see where your priorities lie," Maggie said quietly, raising her brows at Dean before turning to respond to Susie's comment. "We can work out a plan," she continued, and Dean was glad to be out of the spotlight.

"We can't, but it doesn't matter. I won't be doing it. It's fine, I'm not that bothered, honestly," Susie said, her cheeks flushing as she gave Maggie a hard look, as though trying to indicate that her words were final.

Maggie shrugged, completely unmoved and clearly unconvinced about Susie's lack of interest in going. "We have three issues to resolve," she said, ignoring the glare Susie gave her. "Firstly, you'd worry about your mum."

"Well, that's easy," Nathan said. "Maggie and I can pop in to see her and keep her company while you're away."

"Aargh!" a bellowing voice interrupted, and they all stepped apart to allow the boy dressed in a Spiderman costume to race between them, quickly followed by a girl in a mud-covered vest and shorts, waving a foil pom-pom as she went.

Dean watched them go with a smile; it was great to see children enjoying the garden the same way he and his brothers had when they'd been growing up. The large space was meant for families to enjoy, and despite how much work Grace had always put into keeping it beautiful, she'd never minded them racing through the flowerbeds and kicking an endless array of footballs into her sculpted hedges.

"The second issue is your jobs," Maggie said, continuing as if they hadn't been interrupted. "Well, I can get a temp in to cover you in the office. That way, your job would stay open for when you're back, and I'm sure Marsha at the pub would do the same for you."

"I don't want to let you both down," Susie said.

"Giving us notice that you're going away for a couple of months isn't letting us down," Maggie said. "It's being responsible and letting us plan cover."

"That's all well and good," Susie said, cutting Maggie off. "But I still can't afford to stay in London. I've looked into it, and the most I could manage is two part-time jobs around the placement hours, and there's nothing I can do that would pay me enough to cover my bills here and afford to live there." Susie's blush deepened and she looked down, studying her trainers, as though she'd realised just how much she'd given away. It was clear this was something she wanted enough to have explored all her options before giving up on it.

"That's tricky," Maggie said. "I know how expensive it'd be to rent somewhere in London for a few weeks in the summer."

Dean found himself nodding along. Expensive wasn't the word. A short-term rental during peak season would be extortionate — well, if you wanted anything that wasn't a complete hovel anyway.

"Oh my God, I can't believe I didn't think of it earlier," Maggie said, turning to him, her face lit up. "Susie could stay with you." Either oblivious to, or deliberately ignoring, the tightening of Susie's jaw, Maggie continued, "She could have stayed at my place, but the sale was completed a few weeks ago. Your place would be perfect, though. You even have a spare room."

Dean swallowed, his brain racing as he tried to come up with a reasonable excuse to say no. Any kind of excuse would do. The thought of facing the memories he relived every time he looked at Susie on a daily basis made him want to throw up. Sucking in a breath, he realised that after the initial shock of seeing her earlier, he hadn't thought of that night at all. Maybe he could do it. But a couple of hours while surrounded by other distractions was one thing; facing her day after day was something else entirely.

He forced himself to meet Susie's gaze, knowing from her reaction that she didn't want this any more than he did. Perhaps he could just say no?

Despite the redness of her cheeks and the set of her jaw, he caught a glimpse of something he hadn't expected to see; she was nervous. Something that looked a lot like hope flickered across her features before they shuttered again.

"Please don't worry about it," Susie said, before he could open his mouth. "I've absolutely accepted that I can't go, for more reasons than not having anywhere to stay." She glanced across the garden, her posture closing slightly at the sight of the women who'd been gossiping about her in the kitchen.

"Other than the reasons Maggie seems to have solved, what's stopping you from going?" The question slipped out before Dean could stop it. He gave himself a mental slap. He should have just shut up and been grateful for the fact that he'd been saved from having to refuse her, but the realisation that if she didn't take up this placement she'd be exposing herself to even more gossip and judgement seemed to have short-circuited something in his brain.

"Oh, you know," she said, waving her hands around in a way that was familiar to him. "I already work two jobs and I have to help Mum, and I have my university course."

He knew she was studying for some kind of art degree.

"I thought the university said the placement could replace that term's assignments?" Maggie asked.

"Well, they did, but there's Mum, and work," Susie said, shuffling slightly.

"Both of which we've just solved," Maggie said.

Part of him was willing Maggie to shut up and let Susie decide not to do the placement, but Dean realised that the second he'd seen that flicker of fearful hope, he'd decided he'd do whatever he could to help her. He couldn't believe he'd never realised that she'd taken the brunt of the gossip for the accident. The least he could do was save her from more of the same. If that meant he had to spend a couple of months seeing Susie and reliving the most traumatic moment of his life, well, he'd just have to find a way to deal with that.

"So, when are you coming?" Dean asked, raising an eyebrow, and wondering just how much of a glutton for punishment one person could be.

CHAPTER FIVE

Dean watched Hazel as she stroked the length of her immaculate blonde hair, something he knew she did when she was upset.

"So, you won't be coming to my work's do on Saturday?" he asked, mentally working out just how much his colleague Niall was going to tease him about going solo.

"Is that what you're worried about?" she asked him. "I've just said I don't think we're working, and your only concern is whether or not you'll have to go to a function alone?"

Dean didn't answer, knowing that anything he said now was going to be wrong.

"Well, doesn't that just sum up our problems?" Hazel said, tugging on her hair.

He remained silent. Part of him knew he should be persuading her to give things another try, at least until he got past this weekend; after all, she was the perfect date for these things. Not only was she gorgeous in that slightly over-skinny model type way that seemed to appeal to men and women alike, but she was a successful trader, something that he knew was the cherry on the cake in terms of impressing other people. She was exactly the sort of date he should be taking to these sorts of things.

"Why don't you just come anyway? It's a great opportunity to see if we can work things out, and you'd make some good contacts." He'd thrown the last bit in as a final attempt to persuade her. After all, he knew just how important the right contacts were for her to perform well in her job, and she was nothing if not ambitious, a quality he admired.

"I just don't think we're right for each other," she said.

Dean began to tune out. He knew this speech all too well; it was the 'you don't seem that committed' speech that he'd heard enough times for it to be embarrassing. He genuinely didn't know how it always came to this. He deliberately dated the most attractive, successful women he met, the sort who would impress everyone else, and were lovely with it, yet it never seemed to work out.

He began the process of working out how to explain this latest failure to his colleagues. He might have had a lot of girlfriends, and most of the men he knew were jealous of the fact that just about every one of them looked like they could grace a catwalk, but it turned out that being with someone completely gorgeous didn't make him any better at relationships, or getting the women to stay with him long enough for a real connection to develop. One of these days, he'd be enough for someone.

Part of him knew the reason he was tuning Hazel out was to save himself the pain of hearing the same complaints. It was never fun to be told he wasn't trying hard enough, when he truly didn't know how to try any harder.

He couldn't hang around in the concrete car park all day, but he couldn't face the thought of heading back into the office while his emotions were still so raw. At least if he didn't listen to everything she said, he could start trying to pull his veil of confidence back into place while Hazel got everything off her chest.

He vaguely noted a rusty blue vehicle pull into the small car park, but didn't spare it a second glance. He only noticed how out of place it looked amongst the rows of expensive, shiny cars. He realised Hazel had paused and forced himself to pull his attention back to her. He didn't want to be rude, and he certainly didn't want to clue her in on the fact he wasn't listening. That would just set her off on a whole new round of his faults.

"I'm really sorry, Hazel," he said, knowing that his genuine regret was audible.

Why couldn't he make relationships work? Rubbing his hand over his face, he watched until she'd walked out of sight, her hips swaying slightly, accentuating her shapely legs as she went.

Taking a deep breath, he tried to steady his thoughts and turned to head back into the office. They were all working flat out to try to find the glitch that was going to prevent Project Horizon from being released, and he'd been gone too long already.

He'd taken two steps when a gentle cough pulled back his attention. Turning towards the sound, he took in the dodgy blue car that definitely didn't belong in this car park, but it was the sight of Vans trainers leading to slim legs clad in jeans that made him realise he'd just embarrassed himself in front of Susie.

The awkward smile on her face made it abundantly clear that any hope he had that she'd missed the dressing down he'd just received was in vain.

"Sorry about that," he said, rubbing his cropped hair. "My life isn't usually that exciting."

"No problem," she said, the awkwardness melting from her expression. "None of my business, and if it helps, my love life isn't much better."

Susie raised her hands as if trying to calm him, but it was the familiarly mischievous curl of her lip that made Dean smile back. He thought he could hear screeching metal and blinked hard. He wasn't there; it wasn't happening again. It was fine, she was fine.

Sucking in a breath, he forced himself back to the present.

"Is it okay if I get the keys?" Susie asked, seemingly oblivious to his reaction.

Dean glanced at his watch, realising he'd been out here for far longer than intended. Damnit, he was going to get a grilling if he reappeared after all this time, only to disappear again.

"Do you want me to come with you to get them?"

"If you don't mind, that'd be great," he said, shooting her a surprised but grateful smile. "I'm going to be stuck here half the night as it is. I could do without a kicking as well."

"You've definitely changed, then," Susie said. "The Dean I knew would have relished the chance to wind up the boss."

"Yes, I'm a little more focused on keeping my job now."

"Oh dear," Susie said, giving him a faux frown. "That sounds a lot like sensible talk to me."

"Now you're just being insulting," Dean said, grateful for the easy way she had lifted his mood and made him feel lighter than he had in years.

"So, this is where you spend your days?" Susie asked, her gaze wandering over the cubicle he'd made his own. Dean glanced at the space, wondering how it would seem to her. There was the obligatory family photo, but it was tucked away at the back of the desk, half hidden by his array of screens. Otherwise, the space was almost clinical.

"Are you sure you're a programmer?"

He turned to Susie with a frown, partly surprised that she remembered what he did, but mostly confused by the question.

She gestured to his desk before looking him up and down. "Aren't programmers supposed to be surrounded by snacks and energy drinks, and dress in jeans and T-shirts covered in cheese puff crumbs?" Her lips quirked, making it clear she was teasing.

"Not when you're obsessed with your image," Niall's voice piped up, his head appearing from the other side of the blue fabric-covered divider that separated their workspaces.

Dean resisted the urge to roll his eyes. Of course, Niall wouldn't miss the opportunity to meet a woman, and show him up in the same move. "I'll see you when I eventually make it out of here," Dean said as he handed the spare key to Susie, deliberately ignoring Niall.

"Probably not," she said. "I start at that bar today, remember."

Between the emotional discussion with Hazel, and attempting to ignore the way Niall was eyeing Susie over the cubicle dividers, Dean had forgotten that Susie was likely to be out of his flat far more than she was going to be in it. Well, that was good. He didn't have time to deal with the memories all the time.

"Good luck," he said, remembering to be polite.

"I won't need it," she said, giving him the cocky grin that had caused him to follow, and lead, her into no end of trouble when they'd been younger.

Niall stood and leant forward, as though wanting to speak to her, and she turned to him.

"Who needs luck when you're amazing?" she said, making Niall nearly fall over, before turning back to Dean and leaning in close. "Okay, so not strictly true, but I'm pretty sure I can manage making a few drinks," she said, giving Dean a wink before turning and heading out. He smiled more widely than he had in a long time.

CHAPTER SIX

Folding the polo shirt with the Ground Up logo on the front and back and putting it in her large handbag, Susie smiled at Momin, her new supervisor, and owner of the coffee shop where she'd be working four shifts a week while she was in London.

"We're busy from about six-thirty in the morning right through to about seven in the evening. We stay open until eleven, and we need the extra help in the daytime," he explained to her as he tapped away on his phone, finishing the list of her shifts for the next week before hitting send. "We're generally quieter at the weekends as well."

"I guess the offices are busier in the week?" she said, smiling and waving her phone at him to show she had the information.

"Yes, the staff in the businesses around us must have caffeine instead of blood in their veins, but I'm not complaining," Momin said with a smile. "Here, take these," he continued, passing Susie a white box sporting the same black swirl as the polo shirt she'd been given.

"What's that for?" she asked.

"You should try some of our products so you can tell everyone how amazing they are tomorrow," Momin said with a smile.

Opening the box, Susie smiled at the sight of the sweet baked goodies. "Thanks, that's dinner sorted. I'll see you at six in the morning, then?" she asked, trying not to mentally calculate just how little sleep she'd be getting after her training shift at the bar.

"I won't be here, but you'll get to meet my wife Zara," Momin said.

"He'll be too busy baking at that time of the day," said Roman, one of Susie's new colleagues.

"Do you make everything?" Susie asked, studying the display case again.

"Yes, we like to make sure that all of our products are halal," Momin said.

"And you're a control freak about quality," Roman said, grinning.

"Listen to you, you've been here a whole two months and you think you know everything," Momin said.

Roman rolled his eyes. "Am I wrong?"

"Well, no," Momin said with a good-natured shrug.

"You care about your business," Susie said. "That's a good thing."

He gave her an appreciative smile before shooing her out the back. "Go, we'll see you tomorrow."

Stepping out of the café and back into the street, Susie smiled. She was going to like working in the bustling café. Roman's good-natured teasing of their boss made it clear it was a close-knit team.

Balancing the box of pastries and cakes in one hand, and attempting to retrieve the key Dean had given her from the depths of her bag with the other, Susie fumbled, almost dropping the box as she pushed the key into the lock. Swinging the door open, she froze for a moment before grinning. The long corridor was lined with colourful posters of TV shows she remembered watching with Dean into the early hours of the morning.

Easing her suitcase into the hallway, she let the door swing closed behind her and left the case where it was as she made her way to the lounge. The white space was dominated by an enormous TV screen that had half a dozen gaming consoles underneath it. Surprisingly, the wires were neatly organised instead of the nest of tangles she remembered from the bedroom he'd shared with Nathan growing up.

Walking through the space, Susie let herself absorb the atmosphere Dean had created. She'd half expected a place that was bare except for his beloved tech, but he'd made a real home. It didn't have the sort of gentle touches that would have indicated a girlfriend's influence, but it somehow felt welcoming.

The sound of a vacuum cleaner was coming from the corridor that ran off at a right angle to the one she'd entered from. A quick glance at her watch told her it was still far too early for Dean to have come home. Leaving the box of pastries on a countertop, Susie headed towards the sound.

"Hello?" she called.

"Hello." A mop of shaggy brown hair poked out of a door to greet her, shortly followed by the hair's owner. "You must be Susie."

She nodded and gave the young man a cautious smile.

"I'm Dylan," he said, juggling with the vacuum cleaner cable before sticking his hand out.

"Do you live here too?" Susie asked.

"No," Dylan said with a laugh. "A place like this is definitely out of my league. I'm Dean's cleaner."

"But," Susie said, a frown forming on her face, "I was going to clean in return for Dean letting me stay here."

The cheerful smile dropped from Dylan's face. "Does that mean Dean won't want me anymore?" he asked, his brow furrowing. "I kind of need the work, and this job is great cos I can do it around my uni course."

"Oh, no, please don't worry, I don't want to take your job or anything. I'm sure I just misunderstood," Susie said, giving him a weak smile at the realisation that Dean had played her. She'd assumed his silence around her suggestion that she at least contribute by cleaning for him meant he'd wanted to agree but just felt a bit weird about it. It looked like he'd ignored her because he had no intention of letting her do it. She might not like the idea of staying here for free without at least trying to make Dean's life easier, but since she knew first-hand how much people relied on their part-time work, she wasn't about to take that from someone else. She'd just have to figure something else out with Dean.

"So, do you know which room I'm going to be staying in?" she asked, gesturing to the multiple doors along the corridor. Dean had told her his spare bedroom was all set up for her, but she hadn't thought to ask him which room it was.

"It's the one at the end," Dylan said, his spirits revived. "Let me give you the grand tour."

"Bathroom," he said, opening the first door to reveal the modern bathroom, all chrome and white tiles. There was no bathtub, but there was a huge rainfall shower that she couldn't wait to try out.

"Office," he said, moving to the next door. "Well, I think it's supposed to be. I don't clean this room very often as he doesn't really use it, and I'm always worried about messing up all the bits."

The room was sparsely decorated. A huge desk and basic wheeled chair sat with a stack of what looked like computer components on them both. The floor had a spilled pile of technology magazines, but otherwise the small space was empty. The magnolia walls made the light that flowed into the room seem to warm the entire space, making it feel much cosier than it should have felt given how unloved it clearly was.

"This is Dean's room," Dylan said, opening another door to reveal an unmade bed.

The sight made Susie smile as he quickly closed the door again, resisting intruding on Dean's private space for long, despite how much she'd have loved to properly inspect it. It was probably a good thing Dylan was here to stop her from doing just that.

"This is your room," he said, stepping back to allow her to enter.

A single bed took up the bulk of the space, with a few hooks on one wall that were obviously going to have to suffice as her wardrobe while she was staying here. A small set of drawers was squeezed at the head of the bed. As she sank onto the bed to test it, the scent of fresh laundry powder wafted up and she realised Dean must have washed and made the bed for her.

"Dean asked me to make up the bed," Dylan said, eyeing her speculatively. "I don't think he's ever asked me to do that before."

"Well, I really appreciate it," Susie said. "The room looks great."

She smiled to herself as Dylan headed off to finish his work. She was in what was probably one of the smallest bedrooms she'd ever seen, but she was here, she was really doing this. Despite the fact she was twenty-eight, this was the first time she'd been away from home for more than a couple of nights since she was fourteen, and it was certainly the first time she'd done it on her own. Stretching her legs out, she wiggled her toes and grinned at the bare lightbulb hanging from the ceiling.

If she could ignore the fact Dean wasn't letting her pay him anything for staying here, she could convince herself this was what independence felt like.

As she pushed her second suitcase and her portfolio folder through the front door, Susie silently thanked Dean for letting her use his car parking space as well as putting her up. It had been hard enough work getting everything from her car into his flat. The thought of trying to get everything across the country on a train and then across the city without her car would have been enough to put her off attempting the placement completely. The fact he didn't actually have a car, despite owning what she was sure was a very coveted parking space, didn't mean he had to let her borrow it. Yet another thing she would have to find a way to repay him for.

As she started nosing through his kitchen, her phone rang. Realising it was her mum, she picked up quickly.

"Are you okay?" she asked, knowing the distance was going to be hard on Dorothy.

"You've only been gone a few hours. I'm fine," her mum said. "I just wanted to make sure you got there okay."

"Yes, the journey was fine, but Maggie was right. I won't be driving much while I'm here. The last bit as I got into the city was so busy and complicated. I won't be in a hurry to repeat that experience."

"Did you go to the coffee shop? What are they like?"

"Yes, Momin, who owns it with his wife, gave me a quick intro to everyone and how it works. They seem really lovely, and I think I'm really going to like working there."

"But will you be able to manage doing that and working in that pub as well as your placement?"

Susie knew the question came from genuine concern for her wellbeing, but she knew there was a little bit of worry about money as well. "It'll be fine. I normally work two jobs and go to uni, so it won't be any different," she said, concentrating to make sure she kept her tone positive. "I'll make sure to put the money in the bills accounts on time."

"You know you don't have to keep doing that," Dorothy said, her voice dropping.

Susie sank into the couch, marvelling at how comfortable it was as she answered the same way she always did. "I live there too, Mum; I'm supposed to pay my way."

"You do more than pay your way." Dorothy's voice had taken on a melancholy tone that made Susie wish she were there to hug her.

"We're a team, Mum," she said. "Anyway, do you want to know what Dean's flat is like?"

She deliberately changed the subject, knowing her mum, who couldn't pass up a home renovation or building programme, wouldn't be able to resist knowing about Dean's flat. The reality was, Susie did more than pay her way, but there was no way Dorothy could afford even half of the bills and both the mortgages on the house on her own, so Susie used almost every penny she earned to cover the rest, and tried to ignore the amount of debt she was racking up paying for her university course.

Describing the way Dean had made his space both welcoming and personal to him, Susie let the money worries wash away, instead focusing on making sure Dorothy was in a more positive state of mind.

CHAPTER SEVEN

Rubbing her tired eyes, Susie silently wished that sleep featured more prominently in her life as she watched the two other placement students set out expensive-looking art supplies on their designated workstations. She lifted her battered baby blue plastic case onto her own table, determined not to worry about the fact she was carrying what was clearly a cast-off kids' case, and that everything she owned looked as well used as it was. It wasn't as though this was the sort of thing where the quality of your equipment mattered — oh wait, yes it was. Well, there wasn't anything she could do about the fact she didn't have money to spend on new equipment. She'd been one of only three people in the entire country to get this opportunity, and she'd done it with these materials.

Glancing around the massive white room, she allowed herself a deep breath to enjoy the incredible amount of light that flooded the space. The thought of spending the next few weeks here, learning from the man whose art adorned the walls in various stages of completion, was enough to make her forget that she'd been working until the early hours. There was no sign of the man himself yet, but his housekeeper had let her in and she'd been led through the most beautiful Georgian townhouse, and out to this bespoke building in his garden, where she'd found her two fellow students already in situ and setting themselves up.

Placing her array of oils, acrylics, pastels, and pens on the table alongside the brushes and palettes seemed to soothe her, easing her fears about whether she'd measure up to Sam Harrison's expectations. She was determined to make the most of her time here and learn everything she could. Smiling at the two other artists, she moved from behind her workstation and walked over to them. They were both far younger than her, clearly the more traditional age for people doing an art degree, and despite the slightly haughty look the boy gave her, she held her smile. She knew all about wanting to project an image to the world, and she wasn't about to assume the one he was projecting was who he really was.

"Hi, I'm Susie," she said, holding her hand out to shake his.

He stared at it for a beat before raising his own hand and taking hers. "Charles," he said in a voice that dripped privilege, before dropping her hand as fast as possible.

"Nice to meet you, Charles," she said, before turning to the girl. She couldn't have been more different, almost bouncing on the balls of her feet as she waited to introduce herself.

"I'm Laura," she said, shaking Susie's hand vigorously. "I'm so excited. I can't believe I'm here. I was sure he'd only pick people from like, Oxford or Cambridge, or like the Russell Group. I go to Loughborough, and loads of people say it's rubbish, but it's near home so I wanted to go there and I really like it."

Susie smiled at Laura as the girl paused for a breath; she had a feeling she and the bubbly girl were going to get on well.

"I'd like to believe I'm here on merit, not because I go to Oxford," Charles said, his voice cold as he resolutely studied the paintbrush in his hands, flicking the soft bristles back and forth over his palm.

Laura's mouth fell open, her expression dropping instantly. "Oh no, I'm so sorry, I didn't mean that. I was just, well, I don't know. Everyone's always telling me I talk rubbish. I just feel so lucky to be here and I was rambling and, well, now I'm rambling again and I'm really sorry." She moved over to

Charles's side, placing her hand on his, stilling his movements. "Please say you'll forgive me, and we can be friends."

Charles stared at Laura's hand on his for a moment before flicking his gaze to her face; at the sight of her huge blue eyes, wide and pleading, he looked away and blushed a deep red, before clearing his throat and nodding, his eyes fixed back on their connected hands.

Susie supressed the grin that threatened as she took in Charles's complete bewilderment at his obvious and sudden attraction to the freshly cheerful Laura. She was used to being much older than her fellow students — that's what starting a university degree nine years later than normal did — and she always got on well with them, even though her other commitments meant she couldn't indulge in the party lifestyle that accompanied most people's university experience. She was, however, extremely grateful to be bypassing the emotional angst that came with figuring out your own identity at the same time as working through first love. Her first love had been unrequited, and she was forever grateful that he remained unaware of her youthful crush. There was something sweet about seeing it blossom, though. She just hoped Charles wasn't setting himself up for a disappointment that pushed him further into the shell of entitlement that he seemed to have wrapped around himself.

Shaking off thoughts that were definitely too serious for the first morning of her placement, Susie directed the discussion to what kind of art they all preferred. Just as they were discovering that Charles, of course, preferred the classical oil style of painting, and Laura loved the bright impact of acrylics, the sound of the door opening silenced them all.

"I've been doing these things for five years, and you lot are the first to actually start talking before I even get here." Sam Harrison's deep Yorkshire accent seemed to fill the space as he greeted them.

The three of them stiffened and for a beat Susie wondered if she should apologise, but instead, she shrugged and gave him a grin.

"What did the others do, then?"

"No clue, just stood here fiddling with their kit, probably," he laughed, and Susie was pleased to see her fellow students relax.

"Right then," he said. "I've got your portfolios, so I know where you are in terms of your technique and preferences. We're going to spend the first couple of weeks going through the range of techniques and materials that I like to work with. I know you might have covered them, and I know that you probably already think you don't like some of them, or more likely, that you 'can't do them'. It doesn't matter if you can or not; we're going to mess around and have some fun."

Charles shuffled, leaning forward as though about to speak before seeming to shrink back on himself.

"Spit it out, lad," Sam said.

"I thought we were here to learn," he said stiffly.

"Aye, you are," Sam replied.

"How is 'messing around' going to help?"

"Look, I'm not a teacher," Sam said. "I offer these placements because I've been lucky enough to do alright with my career."

Susie snorted.

Sam turned to her, eyebrows raised in question.

"Sorry," she said. "It's just, 'alright' doesn't quite cover your career."

"Fine, I've been bloody successful; doesn't mean I'm soft enough to go on about it."

Unable to stop the laugh that slipped out, Susie was pleased when Sam and the others joined in. She just knew she was going to love this placement.

"Anyway," Sam said, when they pulled themselves together, "I've no doubt you've been learning loads of really important stuff at uni, but what they don't teach you is that you need to mess around; you need to make lots of really awful stuff because you need the confidence to deal with it. Great art, not just good stuff, but really great art means putting yourself out there, letting all your hopes and fears out, all your dreams, and letting other people see them. You can only do that if you let go completely; you can't hold back."

Susie stared at Sam, wondering if the others had been hit as hard by his words as she had. She couldn't breathe, the impact of his statement seeming to punch her right in the chest. Slowly sucking in a lungful of air, she ignored her racing heart.

Almost on autopilot, she followed the others to the front of the room, watching as Sam grabbed a selection of pastel chalks.

"I had an idea at the weekend for an image that brings the feel of being in the front row of a concert to the canvas."

Susie forced her mind to focus on his words as a way to push the panic away. This was what Sam Harrison was famous for: creating works of art that evoked an experience. She needed to concentrate, otherwise she might as well not be here.

As Sam swooped his chalks across the A1 sheet, she realised that she was getting to see something that almost no one else in the world would ever see. She was watching a master at the beginning of his process, and if she was lucky, she'd get to see as this initial idea was developed, made richer and fuller, until the final piece was completed and out in the world.

Turning slightly, she took in the awestruck looks on Charles's and Laura's faces, knowing she wore the same expression.

It was going to be fine; it would be more than fine. She could enjoy this extraordinary opportunity and learn from a world-renowned talent without giving up her hard-won control.

CHAPTER EIGHT

Throwing her jacket on the row of hooks that had remained resolutely empty for the few days she'd been here, Susie paused, wondering whether or not Dean had made it home from work yet. There were no handy signs, like keys thrown on the unit by the door, or shoes left by the mat, but she'd quickly learned that that didn't mean anything. Here or not, he was doing a good job of avoiding her.

She wondered when he'd become such a neat freak. Even his desk at his office had been strictly organised. The Dean she'd known had been a typical young man; the back of his Vauxhall Astra had been strewn with empty food wrappers, and if Grace Parker hadn't been shouting at her son to tidy his room whenever Dean had come sprinting out of the house to greet her, Susie would have worried the woman was ill.

Now, taking in the homely apartment, she wondered why everything was so tidy. If it wasn't for the fact her one glimpse of his bedroom had shown her the sort of mess she'd been expecting, she'd have believed that whatever part of the old Dean the accident hadn't stolen away had been taken by the intervening years. Pushing off one of her trainers with the other heel, and then doing the same with the second one, she made an effort to straighten them, so they at least looked neat, before heading into the open-plan living area.

Usually she dealt with people's attitude to her by being pleasant and ignoring their reservations until they were forced to deal with her. Unfortunately, they had to actually be there for that to work.

A glance at the clock told her it was midnight, but what it didn't tell her was whether Dean was home and asleep, or still at work. He'd already been back later than her a couple of times this week, the sound of him attempting to creep around the place so as not to wake her amusing her enough that she didn't tell him she almost never fell asleep before two a.m. The fact she was awake didn't mean the early hours of the morning were the right time to try to push past his discomfort with her presence, though. There'd be better opportunities, or so she hoped.

Deciding she didn't fancy another night spending hours staring at the ceiling, she grabbed a bottle of beer from the fridge, making a mental note to buy some when she was out tomorrow; she didn't think Dean would mind her borrowing one, but she didn't want him to think she'd take advantage of his hospitality and just take things. It was bad enough that she'd had to accept staying here rent-free.

Popping the lid off, she leant back, taking a big gulp, the longed-for relaxation escaping her at the sound of the front door opening and causing her to spit out her beer in surprise. Leaping up to clean up the mess she'd now made of Dean's immaculate room, she paused at the look of amusement on his face.

"Oops," she said.

"Don't worry," he said, heading to his room and disappearing from sight.

"Okay, that's not rude," she muttered, grabbing a cloth to wipe up her spill. She hadn't seen him since collecting his keys, but given the fact they worked on almost entirely opposite schedules, that at least made a little sense. She wasn't going to worry about the real reason he'd been avoiding her — well, she was, but she wasn't going to let it stop her trying to be friendly.

Using the fact they both worked long hours as an excuse to avoid her was one thing, but walking away the minute he got home to find she was in was bordering on obnoxious. Why had he invited her to stay if it was so difficult for him to be around her? Sitting down again, she grabbed the bottle, determined the next mouthful was going to end up in its proper destination, and huffed.

"That's not a happy sound," Dean said.

Looking up, Susie met his gaze, taking in the dark shadows under his eyes and the air of weariness about him. She realised he'd taken off his jacket, backpack, and shoes. So perhaps he wasn't avoiding her completely, just sorting himself out now he was home.

"You look like you've had a hell of a day," she said, not willing to admit that she'd taken his behaviour personally. In her defence, he'd basically started avoiding her years ago, so it wouldn't have been out of character, but she didn't want him to know she cared, and reacting to something so small would make it obvious.

Grabbing himself a beer, Dean turned and gestured towards her with a bottle; years working behind a bar meant Susie caught his meaning.

"No, I literally just opened this one," she said. "I'll buy some more tomorrow."

"Don't worry," he said. "I'll just add more to the next supermarket delivery."

Of course he didn't need to worry; he probably earned more in a month than she did in a year, but that didn't mean she was about to start freeloading. Susie thought about the amount of time she'd save if she could afford to have her groceries delivered. She wondered how Dorothy was coping without her there.

"I appreciate you letting me stay here, even if you tricked me into thinking I could pull my weight a little bit by cleaning for you, but I'll at least pay my way with food and stuff," Susie said, her tone sharper than she'd intended.

Dean frowned at her for a beat before shrugging. "You wouldn't want Dylan to be out of a job, would you?"

She took a deep breath; he already knew the answer to that. She worked hard enough to make ends meet herself; she wasn't going to take that away from someone else. "So, just how bad has your day been?" she asked, glad he hadn't challenged her on her need to try to retain some independence by at least paying her share of the grocery bill.

"Pretty awful," he said.

Susie just watched him, another trick from her bar work; if you gave people space to talk, they would, and Dean looked like he needed to talk.

"You know I work for a software company?" he asked.

She nodded.

"I'm a senior developer and we're working on a new social media app. I can't talk about what it's for; this stuff is always really confidential. They are so secretive about it even I don't know what they are going to call it; it's just Project Horizon for now."

"That sounds like it should be exciting?"

"It should, but we're due to launch in a couple of months and there's a problem with the beta version. I feel like I'm never going to crack it."

"Ah," Susie said. "I don't think I can help with that."

Dean smiled. "No one can. There are two of us working on it, and we're the only ones who know the coding in enough detail to figure out what the problem is."

"And is the other person any good?"

Dean frowned, rubbing his hand over his cropped hair. "Yes," he finally said.

"Well, that's a good thing because that means there are two experts to solve it."

"How do you know I'm an expert?" Dean asked, and although she couldn't put her finger on it, Susie had a feeling he was asking more than he seemed to be.

"You said 'senior developer'; you must be good," she said with a smile.

Dean smiled back, but it didn't quite reach his eyes. "I'd like to think I am," he said, tipping his bottle.

"I think we both need another one," Susie said, standing and heading over to the fridge.

"Have you settled in okay here?" he asked.

"Yes, thanks," she said, sinking back into the couch after handing him a beer. "You have a lovely place."

Dean laughed as she carefully placed her own bottle on a coaster. "You think it's boring," he said.

"I wouldn't say boring," she said, knowing she'd waited a beat too long to reply. "It's very tidy."

"I suppose you'd have covered the walls in blotches of colour and have a million cushions everywhere," he said with a smile.

His words instantly conjured up an image of her bedroom eight years ago; she'd loved the tie-dye effect he'd helped her to create on her walls and the mountain of cushions that had cocooned her. It had been her happy place.

Susie shrugged, not wanting to admit that she'd painted over it all when he'd left her behind. As though changing the colour of her walls could erase the hurt at realising just how much she'd cared about him in the wake of him ghosting her. She had spent so many years pushing those feelings for Dean away, certain that romance spelled the end of any relationship, that it was only when he was gone that she could admit to herself that she'd been in love with him.

"So, the long hours are to fix the problem with the coding?" she asked, needing to move back to safer territory.

"I really want to fix it this week," he said. "We've got this cocktail thing coming up to celebrate one of the partners retiring, and it's going to be bad enough anyway, going alone. Showing up without having done my job will be a nightmare."

"Didn't Maggie go to those things with you?" Susie asked.

"Yes," Dean said. "She was great; we'd go to each other's work things."

"Do you, um, miss her?" Susie asked, not quite wanting to put the question into words, but finding she couldn't ignore the wistful quality to Dean's tone that didn't quite fit with talking about a woman who was now his brother's fiancée.

"God no," he said, laughing. "Maggie's a brilliant friend, but no, just a friend — well, a sister now, I guess, which is great. No, I just remember how awful these functions were before I had her to come along."

"You could take your girlfriend," Susie suggested, thinking it was highly unlikely he'd found a new girlfriend in the few days since she'd seen him apparently getting dumped, but she wasn't about to assume.

"I think you know first-hand that my last girlfriend isn't very likely to want to help me out," Dean said, tilting his head so it rested on the back of the armchair, exposing his neck.

"When is it?" Susie asked.

"Saturday night," he said, the words quiet and slow, as though someone had switched off the batteries to his vocal cords. She guessed that a sixteen-hour day would do that to someone.

"I could go with you." The words fell out before Susie could consider them, but as she thought about it, she realised it was the perfect solution. She couldn't spend the next few weeks here if he was going to avoid her the whole time, although she acknowledged it was probably a bit arrogant to assume his long hours had anything to do with trying not to see her.

"You?" he asked, his head snapping forward.

Okay, so the tone hurt a little bit, but she wasn't about to give up yet; it was the perfect way to spend time together and try to find a way to co-exist without dealing with their past.

"Yes, me. I can do small talk, and if I can help you out, it'd make me feel better about the fact I'm not paying you any rent while I'm here."

"We've talked about that. You're my guest; you don't need to pay me anything. Besides, don't you have to work?"

"Well, we haven't exactly talked about it. We swapped some emails and you refused to discuss it, but we'll leave that alone as I'm very grateful for it. I don't have to work on Saturday; the pub I'm working at pay a premium for weekend shifts, so they give them to the permanent staff first. I probably won't get many of them while I'm here."

"It'll be a formal do," Dean said, studying the bottle in his hands.

"I do own clothes other than jeans and trainers, you know." Susie rolled her eyes, feeling very grateful that while she did own other clothes, Dean had no way of knowing she hadn't actually brought any of them with her.

His gaze shot to hers. "That's not what I meant; you look perfect whatever you wear," he said, before swallowing and looking away, a pink tinge to his cheeks. "I just meant it'll be boring."

"Look, you don't have to take me," she said. "I won't be offended, but I'm more than happy to come along, boring night and all, and give you moral support."

Dean watched her for a moment as if assessing how serious she was, before nodding his agreement. "That would be great, thank you."

Excellent, she had found a way to start getting Dean over his need to avoid her. Now she just had to figure out how to get an outfit for a fancy cocktail party in two days, without breaking her already fragile budget.

CHAPTER NINE

Knowing he'd need something to get through the evening, Dean rolled his neck as he lifted the whisky he'd poured to his lips. He wasn't sure what had possessed him to agree to Susie's suggestion that she join him tonight. Dealing with the partners was going to be hard enough; the last thing he needed was to be fighting the memories that just thinking of Susie always brought back, and having her in the same room was going to make them impossible to ignore.

Snorting, he took a sip; he knew what had possessed him, and it had everything to do with the fact that, while he'd been halfway in love with the gorgeous teenage Susie, she'd developed into an even more stunning woman. She didn't have the long hair and glamorous clothes that seemed to finish off most women's appeal, but she didn't need them. In trainers and jeans, she was damn good-looking. He suspected that in evening wear she'd make Niall jealous, and after a sixteen-hour day and a bottle and a half of beer, that thought had sealed the deal.

Hearing Susie's door opening, he looked up, wanting to see what she looked like. At the same time, he steeled himself not to see her the way he'd seen her for the last seven years. Taking in the make-up that looked like it had been applied by the artist that she was, his eyes drifted down to the deep red dress that clung to her slender frame, the fitted fabric finishing just below her knees. Her slim, short calves led to a pair of black trainers that glittered in the light from the kitchen spots, and a smile curved his lips.

"I hope the shoes are okay?" she asked. "I didn't have anything else with me that would go with this dress."

Looking up, Dean caught the slight glimmer of anxiety in her expression. She was genuinely concerned about his reaction. "They're perfect," he said. "You look amazing."

"I told you I could wear something that wasn't jeans," she said with a laugh, closing the distance between them and taking the glass from his hand before lifting it to her mouth.

"Are you really telling me you brought a dress like that with you?" he asked. He didn't know that much about fashion, but he'd had enough girlfriends over the years to know that they never packed a dress without packing the accessories to go with it.

"Fine, you caught me — I got it at the Hospice Charity Shop a couple of streets over. They were brilliant," Susie said as she gave him a twirl. "It'll do for tonight."

"It'll definitely do," Dean agreed, his eyes tracking her throat as she swallowed the last of his whisky.

Dean was half listening to Alison as she chatted to him about her children; he liked the company financial controller, and normally loved hearing about the antics of her twin eight-year-old girls, but he kept finding himself searching for Susie. Feeling himself relax as he spotted her chatting to Nigel, the partner whose retirement party this was, he smiled at the realisation she was back over by the floor-to-ceiling windows. He'd known the event was at the Shard, but hadn't thought to mention it to Susie, and she'd looked stunned when she'd realised where they were going.

Since they'd arrived she'd circulated, chatting to people, but kept gravitating back to the windows, as though she couldn't get enough of the view. Part of him was desperate to know what she was talking to Nigel about, but it wasn't because he was worried; he'd quickly realised how good she was at talking to people, getting them to open up and almost blossom under her attention. He just wanted to hear her voice, to be on the receiving end of that attention. Blinking hard, he took a deep breath; what had that been about? He didn't want to be the focus of her attention. If anything, he needed to get back to avoiding her. They'd had a total of three whole interactions in the last week. How, between her collecting his spare keys, one night chatting and tonight, had he stopped seeing what he'd done — specifically, what he'd done to her? He realised that from the moment she'd walked out of her room in that dress, he hadn't seen Susie, the girl who'd been injured in the car accident he would always blame himself for, the girl who'd been with him when he realised he had killed someone that night, the girl he'd hurt. Instead, he'd seen the woman she'd become.

"It was bound to happen eventually," Alison said, laughing as she placed her empty glass on one of the chest-high tables that were dotted around the room, and took another tall glass filled with blue liquid from a waiter who was passing.

Pulling his attention away from something he had no business thinking about, and back to the woman he was supposed to be talking to, Dean blinked and smiled. "What was bound to happen?"

"You, falling for someone," Alison said, tilting her head towards Susie. "You've brought plenty of different women to these things over the years, but I've never seen you look at any of them like that."

"What?" he said. He knew he'd been distracted, which was rude, but he didn't connect to what she was saying. "No, it's not like that. We were really good friends from when we were fifteen until we were twenty-one. I haven't seen her much since then; I was just reflecting on how things change."

"How good?" Alison asked, lifting one eyebrow.

"Just friends," Dean said, wondering why it had never gone any further. At fifteen, he'd thought Susie was gorgeous and she'd been fun. It was just as well that's all they had been; he wasn't sure he could have coped with everything that happened if they had been more.

He glanced back at Susie, the question of why things had stayed platonic ringing through his mind. He didn't know how to answer it. As he watched, she turned, giving the man who had just approached a welcoming smile. Oh hell, no. He wasn't having that. He wasn't possessive by nature, but he wasn't about to let Niall start telling tales to Susie. It was bad enough that he tried to show him up at every turn at work; he wasn't going to start letting the man do it in his private life as well.

"I'll catch up with you later," Dean said to Alison, before striding across the room to Susie. "Niall," he said flatly as he reached Susie's side.

"Hi, Dean, have you tried the martinis?" she asked. "They are amazing. I need to know what they made them with; mine never taste this good."

He shook his head, smiling at her easy enthusiasm. His smile grew as she lifted her glass up to his lips.

"Have a taste," she said. "If you like it, we'll try to grab you one when the waiter comes back around."

Taking her straw in his mouth, he kept his gaze fixed on hers, and a pink blush spread across her cheeks, as though she was just realising exactly how intimate the gesture was.

"You're right, that's amazing," he said, forcing himself to step back after just one sip. "How are you, Niall?" he asked his colleague.

"Great," Niall said, and whatever he was about to follow that up with was cut off as the sound of Elizabeth tapping a glass with a knife rang through the room. The harpist who had been playing in the corner stopped as well.

"Thank you all for coming," Elizabeth began. "It's a bittersweet night for me, well, for many of us at Social Software." Visibly gathering herself, she smiled and continued. "Nigel and I began this company over forty years ago. At that time, the internet was something for obsessives only. In those years, we have seen the world become connected in a way that was unimaginable, even then. We have seen the company we started in the box room of our student flat grow to employ all of you wonderful people, and we have welcomed three other partners to run things with us. I know Nigel's contribution has helped us build a business that will thrive as we each inevitably move on, but we will miss you more than we can say."

Elizabeth wiped the tears that had slipped down her cheeks as she was talking, her immaculate appearance completely unaffected. She patted her greying hair, neatly tucked in its usual twist, before turning to Nigel.

"Thank you, Elizabeth," he said, squeezing her hand briefly before tapping his chest. "I think you know if it wasn't for this faulty ticker of mine, I'd be sticking around for many more years. However, much as I love the company, and all of you, I would rather they didn't have to carry me out in a box."

There was a ripple of laughter around the room, one that would have been much more raucous if everyone present hadn't been aware of just how close Nigel had come to exactly that.

"It has been an honour to work with you all, and I know you will go on to achieve ever more incredible things. However, I would like to think I will be leaving a little gap, and with that in mind, I am pleased to announce that Elizabeth will be responsible for selecting my replacement. Yes, you heard me right: we will be appointing another partner in the next few weeks."

This time there was a gasp, and Dean froze as all heads swung to look between him and Niall. As the two most senior developers, they were the obvious choices. He knew well enough that the other three partners had all come up through the developer ranks, but he'd never imagined he'd have a shot at it himself.

Nigel continued to speak, but Dean couldn't hear him beyond the sound of his blood rushing through his veins. He had a shot at being a partner. The words seemed to loop through his brain. The image of telling his parents rushed to the front of his mind. This was the sort of news that could wash everything else away. It was the sort of dream news that would finally make him good enough.

He and Niall exchanged a look full of understanding. He might not have the best relationship with Niall, but right now, the man was the only other person who would understand what he was thinking, because Niall was thinking it all too.

Finally, the speeches finished, the harpist began playing and chatter filled the room once more.

"Did you know I found the glitch in the code that was causing the log-in issues?" Niall said, breaking into Dean's thoughts.

Dean let the words sink in, and with them the implication.

"Oh, is that the problem you were talking about?" Susie asked, turning back to Dean, a slight frown on her face.

"It's one of them," Dean said, focusing on not letting the dark cloud that had descended in that instant show. There was still plenty for him to do, and he should just be grateful that things were getting fixed, but the way Niall seemed to beat him to it each time drove him mad. Having your face rubbed in the fact you were second best all the time was hard to take under normal circumstances; now, it was a clear, 'I'll be a partner and you won't' taunt, and it was all Dean could do to keep his expression neutral. "When did you manage that?"

"Today. I was working on it this morning and *boom*, fixed."

How the hell did the guy keep doing it? Every time they hit a brick wall, he'd work on it away from the office and fix it. Maybe the change of scenery worked for Niall in a way it didn't work for Dean. It certainly didn't make his chances of becoming a partner look good. "Well done," he said, his excitement over the partnership opportunity flickering and dying.

"Oh, here," Susie said, breaking into the conversation. "I grabbed this for you from a waiter while they were doing the speeches."

Taking the martini glass from her, he felt a chink of light break into his mood; it was nice to have someone looking out for him.

"Thanks."

"I thought you'd have brought Hazel tonight," Niall said, a twist to his lips that was obviously meant to make him look interested, but just made him look sly.

"We broke up," Dean said, grateful that Susie really was just his friend, because if she'd been his new girlfriend, Niall's effort to stick the knife in might actually have worked.

"Who have you come with, Niall?" Susie asked, tilting her head to one side, her voice lifting to a tone that Dean completely forgotten, but recognised in an instant.

"Oh, I came on my own tonight," Niall said, his stilted tone giving away the fact that he hadn't expected to be questioned himself and really hadn't wanted to admit that.

"Oh, I'm so sorry," Susie said, touching Niall's arm, her forehead furrowed.

Taking in the way she studied Niall, her blue eyes unnaturally wide in a way he knew she made them when she was attempting to look innocent, Dean tightened his jaw, determined not to let the smile that was pulling at his mouth slip out. Susie might have grown up, but she was still a firecracker who didn't let people get away with anything.

"Well, I've met you, so it's lucky I did," Niall said, his gaze dropping to Susie's small hand on his arm.

"It's been lovely to meet you too," she said, smiling at him as she dropped her hand, but instead of letting it fall to her side, she slipped it around Dean's waist and eased closer to him. For a beat, Dean's entire body focused on the sensation of heat radiating from her into him at every point their bodies were connected. She was just the right height for her head to tuck under his chin, and if he turned slightly, he would be able to pull her flush against his chest. Only the fear of her pushing away stopped him from giving in to the impulse. The slight drop in Niall's expression only made the pleasure even sweeter.

"How about we go and find someone who can tell us how they made these martinis?" Dean asked.

The beaming smile Susie gave him hit him straight in the chest, and he realised just how much he'd missed being around her. After the accident, he'd felt as though cutting himself off completely had been the only way to cope, but had he been right?

CHAPTER TEN

"I'm sure you have better things to do than traipse across London with me," Susie said to Dean, as they walked through the Tube station entrance, both swiping their Oyster cards as they passed through the barrier.

Her battered black portfolio jamming her in place for a beat as the gust of wind from the Hammersmith station line whipped it sideways meant she missed Dean's reply. She hated lugging the thing around, but she figured she might need it to carry supplies back from her shopping expedition.

At her blank look, Dean repeated himself. "After last weekend, I definitely owe you; helping you carry some shopping back home isn't too much of a hardship."

Hearing him refer to his flat as home gave her a warm glow; she had never lived anywhere except the small semi-detached house she still shared with her mum, and she was surprised to find she'd settled into Dean's flat so quickly. It wasn't exactly cosy, but over the last couple of weeks she'd begun to feel comfortable there — something she was sure had a lot to do with the fact Dean didn't seem to be trying to avoid her anymore.

Slipping onto a train just before the doors whooshed closed, they dropped into a couple of spare seats — a benefit of living towards the end of a line. One line change later and they emerged from the steel and glass block that made Tottenham Court Road station instantly recognisable. Susie took a moment, slightly overwhelmed by the chaos that greeted them. In every direction, pedestrians battled with cars and the iconic black cabs and red buses, and roadworks and construction activity seemed to be dotted around, adding to the general sense of no one quite being in control. She realised that although she knew the address of the shop Sam had recommended for picking up more supplies, she had no idea which direction to go in.

Smiling, Dean took her hand in his. "This way, stay close," he said, moving away from the exit of the station, where they were getting buffeted by the throng of people emerging.

Shopping in London on a Saturday probably wasn't to be recommended if you weren't a tourist, but Susie had been busy between work and her placement all week, so it was today or not at all.

Focusing on the pleasant tingle that spread through her hand and up her arm at the feel of Dean holding on to her, she tried to ignore the bumps and knocks of people pushing past as they made their way through the crowds. Finally, they were far enough down the road that there was space for people to keep a decent distance from each other, and the tightness in Susie's chest eased. Having lived her whole life in a rural Somerset village, she couldn't imagine getting used to this. Looking at Dean, she realised she might be alone with that thought. It seemed he'd made the transition to the city successfully, and she wondered whether it had taken all these years, or if he'd felt comfortable here from the beginning.

"I think this is the place," Dean said, gesturing to a rainbow-coloured sign sandwiched between an electrical store and a furniture shop, the former crammed with white goods and the latter looking as though it had barely any stock, with everything spread out in a way that made it clear very few people could afford what they were selling. Susie knew that Tottenham Court Road was famous for both types of shops, but seeing it for herself made her pause and take a breath. She was going to make the most of her new adventure.

Smiling at the sign, she nodded.

Dean pushed the door open, letting go of her hand to do so, and she instantly missed the contact. Following in his wake, she slipped into the narrow aisle, the sound of the bustling street fading away as the door swung closed behind them.

Taking a deep breath, she let the familiar scents wash over her, her shoulders easing down. There was something special about the way different bases mingled with the scents of oils, watercolours and chalks, the slight tang of primers and varnishes cutting through them all.

"This is your happy place, then?" Dean asked with a smile.

"I've never been here before," she said, not really concentrating on the question as her eyes scanned the shelves and display racks.

"Not this shop specifically, just art shops in general," he said, running his fingers along a shelf filled with tubes of oil paints.

"Yes," she said, the word coming out on a contented sigh.

"I can understand that," he said. "It's like when I'm looking at components, or a base code."

Susie turned away from the pastels that had caught her eye and tilted her head.

"You know," he continued, "it's all possibility and excitement; there isn't any pressure to create something yet, just the pleasure of potential."

Susie stared at him and he looked away, his cheeks colouring as he moved further into the shop. She couldn't stop the dumbfounded expression she was sure was on her face. No one ever understood her fascination with a new sketchpad, or a new tube of paint, a new set of charcoals — she wasn't even sure she understood it herself. She'd always thought it was because she had to work so hard to afford any of it. She'd thought her fascination with supply shopping and having something new was just the pleasure of retail therapy, until now. In one sentence, Dean had peered into her soul.

Snapping her jaw closed, she shrugged off the desire to hug him and tell him just how deeply he understood her. She wasn't about to make a total prat of herself. Instead, she squared her shoulders and followed him further into the narrow but deep space.

"Good morning. Can I help you find anything?" A young blonde woman with a vibrant pink streak in her hair smiled welcomingly at Dean.

"I'm just here to help carry things," Dean said with a chuckle, nodding to Susie to let the woman know she was the customer.

"Ah, we have a couple of armchairs in the corner there if you get bored while you wait," she said, flashing a brilliant smile at him before turning the same smile to Susie. "What are you looking for today?" she asked.

"I have a huge list of things," Susie said, "but I'm not sure I'll be able to afford everything on it. Would it be okay if I have a nosy around and figure out what to go with?"

"Of course," the woman said. "I'll be right here if I can help you find anything. Do you want to leave your portfolio here? It'll probably be easier to have a good look at things without worrying about it."

"I'll try not to be too long," Susie said, turning to Dean.

"Don't rush. I'm glad of the excuse not to be glued to my computer, and I'll be happy to relax over there," he said, gesturing to the battered brown leather armchairs tucked into a corner of the shop.

Relieved he didn't mind, but determined not to take advantage of his good nature, Susie began searching for the items on the list Sam had given her. He'd made it clear to his three students that they didn't need to get everything on the list, and that it was in order of priority, but he'd also made it clear that the more of the items they had, the more they would get out of their placement.

Susie knew there was no chance of her being able to afford everything on the list, despite Sam advising her that this shop was a lot cheaper than most, and the fact she'd marked off the items she already had. Looking around, she wished, not for the first time, that she had a bigger budget. Shaking off the pointless thought, she enjoyed browsing everything the shop had to offer. Having finally forced herself to make some selections in acrylics and inks, she headed towards the brushes, her fingers caressing a Kolinsky sable inkbrush set with beautifully ornate ferrules. She loved the way the beautifully decorative metal connected handle to bristles and longed to touch them but couldn't bring herself to risk spoiling them for whoever did have the money to buy them.

"What are those?" Dean asked, his voice so close to her ear that it made her jump.

"Inkbrushes," she said wistfully, before turning to face him.

"Aren't all brushes the same?" he asked. "Well, you know, once you account for the sizes?"

"To a point. There's a lot of variety in quality, though," she said, thinking how best to explain. "You get a range of synthetic and natural fibres, and they all give a slightly different finish to the work. I guess it's a bit like your computers; they all do the same basic thing, but there are variations in just what you can achieve on them."

Dean grinned at her analogy. "So, these brushes are like my dream machine?" he asked, peering at them.

"Yes, although you can get similar quality for a lot less, these look beautiful as well," she said, trying to convince herself she definitely didn't need them.

"Things that make you enjoy your time are worth a premium," he said, studying her in a way that made her squirm.

"Well, not today they aren't," she said with a smile. "Sorry I've been so long; I've got everything I need, so I'll just go and pay."

"Are you sure?" he asked. "I wasn't trying to rush you; I just wanted to see how you were getting on."

"No, I'm good. I'll be eating beans for the rest of my stay with you if I spend any more now," she smiled at him, letting him know she was teasing, even if she knew her words were closer to the truth than she wanted to admit.

He studied her for a beat, as though debating whether to say something, before nodding. "Fair enough," he said. "I'll come and help you with your bags."

Leaving the art shop with less than Dean was expecting Susie to have purchased given the size of the list he'd glimpsed, Dean realised he didn't want their trip out to end. He wasn't ready to head back to the flat and spend the rest of the weekend with his head stuck in code for Project Horizon.

"Shall we get some lunch?" Susie asked. "I'm starving."

"That sounds great," he said, "but it'll be a nightmare getting a table around here on a Saturday."

"I have an idea, if you don't mind a bit of a walk?" she said, studying the map app on her phone.

Dean nodded. Susie took them off Tottenham Court Road, and he took the carrier bags from her hand, leaving her with her oversized black portfolio case, the one she had refused to let him carry on the way to the shop. She weaved them through the back streets until they emerged on Euston Road, right next to Great Portland Street underground station.

"Wait here," she said, placing the portfolio case on the floor at his feet. "I'll be back in a minute."

He grinned as Susie emerged from the supermarket a few minutes later, waving a carrier bag at him.

"Lunch," she said, picking the portfolio case up and heading away from him before he could respond.

He grinned to himself at the thought of taking any of his recent dates for supermarket sandwiches in the park. Spending time with Susie was definitely refreshing.

As they wound around the station building, Regent's Park came into view. Crossing the road, Dean resisted the urge to grab Susie's hand and make sure she was safe. She was nearly thirty, and more than capable of crossing the road, but the sheer volume of cars moving in all directions made his chest tighten. He needed to get a grip; the busy roads of the city hadn't bothered him before, but then he hadn't had Susie at his side before. By the time he had talked himself out of his need to try to protect her, they had walked through the Outer Circle entrance. He turned to watch as a smile transformed her features, as though the sun had only just emerged.

"I thought we should have a picnic," she said, delight clear in her tone as her head swivelled to take in the sight of the park spreading out ahead of them. "But I didn't realise how amazing this place would be."

"I haven't had a picnic in years," Dean said, taking in the haven of nature in the city. "If you fancy it, we could go for a stroll through Queen Mary's Gardens and see the roses. Apparently, this is the best time to see them in full bloom."

As Susie turned her head back to him, her lips curled in amusement. "I wouldn't have taken you for a flower enthusiast," she said.

"Okay, I have to admit, I only know because one of the customer service guys at work is always talking about plants and said he'd like to come and see the park this weekend."

"Oh, were you planning to come anyway?" she asked.

"It hadn't crossed my mind to come by myself," he said, realising that he couldn't remember the last time he'd planned to go and do something just for the pleasure of it.

They found a less crowded spot of grass, not an easy feat on a sunny June day in one of the busiest cities on the planet, and sank onto it. Susie grabbed the bag of food and started poking through it.

Head popping up, her gaze met his. "Which one do you want?" she asked, holding up a packet of tuna and cucumber sandwiches and a packet of BLT.

Dean froze, the sight of the tuna ones reminding him of her obsession with the stuff. "Do you still love tuna?"

Susie studied him as though stunned that he'd remembered, and he began to squirm. "I do, but I like both, so you can pick," she finally said.

"Like or love?" he asked with a smile. "Because I seem to remember someone loving anything with tuna."

"I don't think 'loved' does it justice. I was obsessed," she said with a laugh. "Do you remember that time I wrestled Joe for the last tuna sandwich at your granny's birthday party? I got it in the end, though."

"I don't think he put that much effort into winning," Dean said with a laugh. Despite the fact Joe was five years younger, he'd already been bigger and stronger than Susie at the time. Dean had thought his youngest brother had protested his desire for the sandwich a little too strongly, and he'd definitely let the playfight go on longer than needed, given that he'd let Susie win anyway.

Leaning back, Dean tuned out the muffled sounds of traffic and let Susie's laugh curl around him. Taking a bite of his sandwich, he realised he couldn't remember the last time he'd felt so relaxed.

CHAPTER ELEVEN

Wiping the counter in what felt like the first lull in custom for hours, Susie acknowledged why Li Jun, her supervisor at the bar, paid a premium for Wednesday evening shifts. The place had been as rammed since she'd clocked on at six p.m. as she'd have expected on a weekend, so much so that the familiar ache in her left thigh was as intense as she could remember it being for ages.

"You look far too happy for someone who's four hours into an eight-hour shift," Li Jun said, swiping the silky jet-black fringe out of his eyes for what had to be the millionth time that night.

"It's been a good few days," Susie said, feeling her lips spread at the memory.

"Today involved being at this madhouse for six p.m. I find it hard to believe your week could be that good. I suspect it was a person, rather than the days."

Despite the fact she'd only worked here for two weeks, Susie had quickly realised that Li Jun managed the pub with a relaxed manner that belied how organised, efficient, and in control of everything he was, and the fact he was so perceptive made it obvious how he pulled it off.

"Maybe," she said, winking as she turned to face the customer who'd squeezed between the people propping the bar up as they chatted and sipped their drinks.

Pulling his already loose tie even further, the man ordered three pints and three Jägerbomb chasers without looking up from his wallet. Susie definitely missed the Angel Arms. The pub she'd worked at in Honeyford was all about chatting to the customers and building rapport. Not that she was complaining; the fact she'd been able to secure two part-time jobs to fit around her placement was a miracle.

After handing the man his change, with him still not even glancing at her, she turned back to Li Jun.

"What's their name?"

Susie smiled at the carefully worded question. One of the benefits of being in the city was that everyone had caught up with the fact there wasn't a default gender. "I've just had a great few days," she said. "You know Dean, the guy I'm staying with?"

"The old friend from home?"

"Yes. At the weekend, we went to pick up some art supplies I needed, then we had a picnic in Regent's Park."

"Oh, that's a real tourist spot," Li Jun said. "Did you see the open-air theatre?"

"Yes, it looks amazing. I'm really hoping I'll get to see a show while I'm here."

"Good luck getting tickets!" he said, tilting his head to let her know he was off to serve someone further down the bar.

At around eight-thirty, Susie glanced up, surprised to see Dean come into the bar with a group of people, some of whom she recognised from the retirement party. She knew he'd been planning to meet some friends that evening, but she hadn't expected them to come here. He waved at her in greeting, but it was almost eleven by the time he approached the bar and she was free to serve him. He gave her that warm smile that barely curled his lips, but radiated from his eyes, despite the tiredness that seemed to pull his shoulders down.

"Here," she said, passing him a martini. "It won't be as good as the ones at Nigel's retirement party the other week, but they are getting better."

"Thanks," Dean said, grinning and pushing a twenty-pound note over the bar.

"No, it's on me," she said.

"It sort of defeats the point of you working here if you're just going to pay for everyone's drinks yourself," he said with a smile, pushing the money across the mirrored surface of the bar.

"Not everyone's, just yours, and you look like you really need it."

Looking at the shadows under his eyes and the tension he seemed to be carrying around permanently now, Susie meant every word. Dean had seemed to relax when they'd lain in the sun eating their lunch on Saturday, but it didn't seem to have lasted into the week.

"Well, with compliments like that, I'll accept. I definitely deserve it now!"

His smile stopped her from trying to apologise. "Oh stop, you know you're as hot as ever. You just look like you've had a rough few days, which you have."

He glanced up from his pint and stuffed the note in the tip jar, and the twinkle that had been missing from his expression was back in place. "You think I'm hot?" he asked.

Rolling her eyes, Susie moved to serve the next person at the bar. It might only be a Wednesday night, but a pub in the heart of London was never quiet. The after-work crowd had been flooding in for the last few hours and now they had settled in, it was only a matter of time before they started winding up for the night.

After whipping up half a dozen Manhattans for a trio of men with carefully sculpted mirror-image beards, Susie moved back to Dean.

"Have you eaten?" she asked, gesturing at his half-empty pint glass.

"No," he said. "I'll grab something on the way home later."

She smiled and passed him a bag of vegetable crisps. "Eat these for now, they'll help."

"Not everyone needs to eat as often as you do, you know," he said, but tore the bag open anyway.

"True, but I'm not the one on my fifth pint."

"Fair enough, but doesn't this place have any normal crisps?"

"Nope, it's all city fancy here," she said with a laugh as he studied the crisps with suspicion.

"So, back to our earlier discussion," Dean said, arching an eyebrow as he looked up from his bag of crisps. "You think I'm hot?"

"You know you're hot," Susie said with a shake of her head. "You don't need me to tell you."

"Damn, I must have grown into it, because you never thought I was hot before."

She smiled at him, knowing he was fishing. He knew perfectly well that teenage Dean had been pretty hot too. There'd been enough girls chasing after him then that he couldn't have had any doubt about it, although he'd definitely grown into the broad shoulders and tall frame that had edged towards gangly when they'd been younger. The strong jaw and serious eyes so light they were almost turquoise were somehow enhanced by the lines that were mere hints on his face.

"Are you having fun?" she asked, changing the subject.

"I guess," he said. "They're a nice bunch, mostly."

"They look like they're celebrating," she said, gesturing to the group he'd arrived with.

"Niall managed another breakthrough on our coding issue. There's still a way to go, but it's a huge step forward."

"You don't look too happy about it."

"I am, of course I am," Dean said, rubbing his jaw.

"It's just Niall being Niall?" Susie surmised.

He shrugged. "He's a good guy, talented."

"Talented at winding you up, maybe."

"No, he's talented. It's not his fault I struggle with him sometimes."

Susie leant forward, resting her hand on Dean's arm. "He's not a good guy," she said.

"He is; it's just my luck that we're up for the same promotion."

"Trust me," she said, holding his gaze and making sure he was focused on her words. "You're amazing for not wanting to judge people. I've spent enough years dealing with people judging me for my father's actions to know how awful it is, but that man enjoys winding you up."

Observing the way Dean seemed determined to see the best in other people, Susie wanted to wrap her arms around him and stop anyone from taking that away from him. Unfortunately, it meant he was being taken advantage of, and that was something she couldn't bear to witness.

"Susie," the man in question said, drawing her and Dean's attention.

"What can I get you?" she asked, summoning a smile she didn't feel for Niall.

After he rattled off his order, which seemed to consist of the most complicated drinks for everyone they were with, she busied herself preparing everything, doing her best to listen to the conversation he was having with Dean. Unfortunately, the noise in the place meant she only caught the odd word. What she didn't miss was the way Dean's smile didn't quite reach his eyes, or the way Niall seemed to puff up further the longer he spoke to Dean.

Almost finished, she spotted a woman walking over to the pair. Tall, with hair cascading down her back, her gaze was almost laser-focused on Dean.

"Buy me a drink," the woman said to Dean, smiling in a way that made it very clear she felt a drink was only the start of things.

Of course Susie heard that, the embarrassing sound of a woman about to get turned down.

"What are you drinking?" Dean replied with a glance over the woman's shoulder at a stunned-looking Niall.

"Whisky, straight," she said, and Dean nodded to Susie, indicating for her to serve the drink.

Susie's jaw tightened as she nodded. Finishing serving Niall, she took comfort in the fact the guy was looking a little less full of himself. At least there was some benefit to Dean getting chatted up.

Susie took Dean's money and sorted his change. She turned to hand it back to him as the blonde slipped onto the stool next to him. Resting her hand on Dean's arm, the woman pulled his attention to her.

A strange pang washed through Susie at the sight. If Hazel was anything to go by, the woman was exactly Dean's type: tall, leggy, large breasts and long hair. She half wished she could say the woman was all make-up and plastic surgery, but she wasn't; she radiated a natural beauty that seemed a great match for Dean.

Passing him his change, Susie gave him an encouraging wink before turning away and leaving him to enjoy the attention, something he didn't look at all unhappy about.

By the time Saturday rolled around again, Susie was grateful it was her day off from all of her jobs, she needed the time to work on her placement pieces. Sam wanted each of them to try to create at least half a dozen different works during their placement, with a view to the best being selected for a show at the end of it. If any were good enough, that was.

Flipping through her pad to look at the part images on each page, Susie realised she needed to start on a full-size image if she wanted to make any use of today. Slipping off her bed, she ignored the familiar twinge in her thigh. Hopefully, a day not on her feet would ease it up. She paced through Dean's apartment, wanting to check he wasn't in before spreading her equipment out.

She wanted to respect the fact he liked to keep his home so spotless, but it wasn't particularly conducive to being an artist. She had half a dozen canvases propped up against the wall in the spare room she'd made her own for the next few weeks, and she'd already managed to get paint on her clothes and smear the work twice. An unfortunate consequence of the fact that the only space big enough for her to lean her work against was also the wall that operated as her wardrobe.

Lifting the piece that she'd barely started but needed to make some decent progress on, and soon, she eased it out of the room and into the lounge area before heading back to her room to gather the plastic case that contained her materials.

Spreading out on the lounge floor, she blasted Bruce Springsteen from her phone. Contentment settled over her as she let herself get lost in the work. Before she knew it, she had filled the sheet with an image of wings that spread across the whole space, creating a feathery effect that hinted at being caught mid-flight.

"Wow." Dean's voice broke her concentration.

Glancing around to take in the mess she'd created, Susie winced. "I'm sorry, I thought you were out for the whole day." He frowned, and she realised that she'd made it sound like he shouldn't be in his own home. "Sorry, I didn't mean that you had to let me know if you plans or anything," she said. "I just … well, I wouldn't have taken up all this space if I'd known you were around today."

"Do you need this sort of space to work?"

"Well, yes, sorry. I won't do it again, though," she said.

Dean turned his frown back to her. "But you need to work on your art, don't you?"

"Yes, but I don't have to do it here," Susie said, her embarrassment easing as she realised with surprise that she wasn't even a little bit uncomfortable at him seeing her unfinished work. Normally, she hated people seeing her work in progress, and quite often felt awkward even once it was finished, but she didn't seem to mind Dean seeing it at all.

"It's incredible," he said, kneeling next to her as he took the time to really inspect what she'd done. "It looks so real, and yet, not," he said, his words hushed. His fingers stretched out, as if to touch the image, but stopped, hovering just above it.

She watched his face as he studied her work.

"You were always talented," he said. "But this is a whole other level."

The sincerity of his words touched her, and she smiled, not feeling the usual urge to explain what was wrong with what she'd drawn, or why it wasn't good enough. She just let herself enjoy his admiration. "Thank you."

He turned towards her, making her realise just how close they were. Her breath caught.

She blinked and looked away. She'd spent enough years when she was younger ignoring her attraction to Dean. It had taken her a long time to accept that just because her dad had let her mum down, it didn't mean that all relationships were doomed to fail, but she'd also spent long enough getting over Dean that she wasn't about to head down that road again. She'd be happy just to have his friendship back and get him to move past any lingering resentment about making him go out that night.

"You need a proper space to work while you're here," he said, standing and holding his hand out to her.

Susie placed her palm in his and let him pull her to her feet. Without letting go of her hand, he led her down the hallway to the door that she knew held his office.

Opening the door, he flicked the light on, dispelling the gloom from the threatening rain outside. "It wouldn't take much to clear this room so you could use it while you're here," he said, gesturing to the stacks of magazines and piles of plastic and wires.

"I can't do that; it's your office," she said.

"Have you seen me use this once since you've been here?"

Her forehead crinkled. He was right, she hadn't seen him use it at all. The couple of times he'd been working at home he'd sat with his laptop at the breakfast bar in his kitchen or on the couch with his laptop connected to the massive TV screen.

"But…" she began.

"No buts," he said. "Let me do this for you."

She studied his face, trying to sense how serious he was, before nodding. "Thank you," she said, before trying to break the tension that had built between them by adding, "Is this just so I don't mess up your lounge?"

"You caught me," he said with a grin.

Studying the room, Susie realised that she'd never imagined having the luxury of a dedicated space for her art. She might have teased Dean about him hating mess, but she knew there was more to it than just wanting his home to look tidy. He'd understood what she needed and gone out of his way to get it for her. The gesture reminded her of the boy who'd done the same thing when she'd been betrayed by her father. Dean had done everything he could to ease her hurt then, and it seemed he was still trying to make things better for her. She squeezed his hand, wanting him to know she appreciated him, but knowing she wouldn't be able to speak around the regret for their lost years that tightened around her chest.

CHAPTER TWELVE

After helping Susie move her work into his rarely used home office, Dean had been ready for it to be Monday. He needed to get away from her for a while. He needed relief from the guilt that seemed to hit him in waves in her company. She didn't seem to hold any kind of grudge about the accident, but that just made him feel even worse.

"How's your lovely house guest?" Alison asked, pausing beside his desk.

"Who's your house guest?" Niall asked, his head popping up from his own cubicle.

"Susie. You met her at Nigel's retirement," Alison said, filling Niall in on something Dean would have much preferred he didn't know.

"She's moved in with you?" Niall said, his brows rising. "That's fast work, even for you."

"She's just visiting," Dean said with a sigh, half wanting to just let Niall believe he had that sort of relationship with Susie.

"So, she's not your girlfriend?" Niall asked, looking thoughtful.

"Well, she's a girl, and she's my friend," Dean said, realising that it was true. Somehow, despite his fears about having Susie around full-time, she'd worked her way back into his affections. Actually, he realised, he'd never stopped caring about her, and that was why he hadn't been able to face seeing her.

Niall's face lit up, and Dean resisted the urge to warn him off. It wasn't his place, even if the voice inside his head was protesting loudly that it should be.

"Ah, so you're single again," Niall said. "That's a shame."

"Not quite," Dean said, not sure where the words were coming from, but knowing he didn't like the smug look on Niall's face. He didn't know why the guy bothered him — it wasn't like he had a great track record himself — but he didn't like the idea of being judged for his relationship status. "I met a great woman at the weekend."

"Really?" Niall said.

"Yes, she's gorgeous and she's an Instagram influencer," Dean said.

Niall's eyebrows nearly disappeared under his floppy hair. "Sure," he said with a laugh.

"Oh, I really liked Susie. I think you'd be good together," Alison said, looking slightly disappointed.

"She's an old friend, that's all," Dean said, and to prove his point, he picked up his phone and sent a text to Lydia, the woman he'd recently met at the bar.

Fancy meeting for that drink later? Would be great to get to know you better, Dean x

Perhaps going out with Lydia would help him shake the weird feeling. Almost instantly she replied, accepting, and naming a place that he knew cost a small fortune just to get in.

"See, date tonight," he said with a grin, waving his phone at the pair.

The day dragged after that, and by the time six-thirty arrived, Dean was beginning to wonder why he'd bothered setting up the date with Lydia. Sure, she was great in all the ways that mattered, but he couldn't seem to find any enthusiasm for the evening ahead. He gave himself a quick once-over in the toilets, before heading down to the Tube to make his way over to the wine bar she'd named. He might not be feeling very enthusiastic, but he would at least do her the courtesy of not being late.

"Hello, handsome," Lydia greeted as he arrived. Dean was surprised to find her already there.

"Hello, lovely to see you again," he said, leaning down to kiss her proffered cheek. "Can I get you a drink?"

"They'll come over once we're settled," Lydia said.

"Is this table okay for you, Miss Starling?" the waiter asked, walking over to them as soon as Dean took his seat in the courtyard booth.

"Yes, it's wonderful. Thank you so much for letting me try so many," she replied with the sort of smile that Dean realised probably got her anything she wanted.

Dean let his attention wander to the courtyard, where every wall was covered in some kind of creeping plant that was in full bloom with pink flowers. The whole place was like a tropical hideaway, no detail too small to complete the effect. He found himself thinking how much Susie would enjoy it.

"I know it's annoying," Lydia said, turning to Dean with a self-depreciating smile, "but I have over three million followers. It's important to ensure I have the best spots for selfies to keep the engagement up."

As she began to explain how she'd set out to build a platform big enough to attract sponsorship and advertising money, Dean smiled at her. It would be so easy to dismiss her and her career as vacuous, especially when she insisted on taking hundreds of shots of them both, and her alone, before she even took a sip of her elaborate cocktail, but there was something genuine and engaging about her.

"I am really careful about the brands I work with," she said. "I only deal with companies with highly diverse boards, and who have an agenda that fits with my focus on female empowerment."

Dean nodded, impressed.

"What about you?" she asked. "I seem to remember you saying you work in social media as well."

"More the software development end of things than the public-facing side, though," he said with a grin.

Their food arrived, distracting him from the conversation, and he waited patiently while Lydia snapped their meals. Once she was happy she had useable shots, he watched her edit them and post a couple of shots to her page. He was pleased to see that she hadn't ordered a plain salad, something that seemed to be a first date rule with women.

"Regular posting helps keep my followers engaged. Anyway, back to you," she said, tucking into her steak with a relish that reminded him of the way Susie attacked her food.

The following morning Dean sat in his cubicle, head between his hands. The date had gone well, Lydia had been good company, and she was gorgeous, so why wasn't he feeling better about it all?

"Come get a coffee with me," Alison said, standing next to him, purse in hand.

Dean glanced at his screen. There was still so much to fix, but he'd been less than useless so far today. Maybe a break would do him good.

Nodding, he stood and followed Alison to the lift.

"Date didn't go so well?" she asked him once they were in the lift.

"That's the thing," he said, frowning. "It went really well; she was funny, nice, successful and gorgeous."

"So, why aren't you happier?" Alison asked.

"I don't know," Dean said. "A guy would have to be crazy not to be excited to go on another date with her."

"But you're not?" she asked, giving him a look that made it perfectly clear she knew the answer to her question.

"No," he said, sighing. "I don't know what's wrong with me," he added, as they walked into the coffee shop situated on the ground floor of the building.

Spotting Susie behind the counter, he straightened. At least there was one bright spot in his day he thought as he gave her a broad smile.

"Maybe you're dating the wrong woman," Alison said, looking pointedly from him to Susie and back again.

Dean rolled his eyes and decided to ignore Alison's efforts at matchmaking. Susie was his friend, and he realised as he said it that it was true. The years he'd spent away from her didn't seem to have changed that.

CHAPTER THIRTEEN

Susie floated into Sam's studio that afternoon, smiling to herself at the sight of Charles gazing wistfully at Laura's currently empty desk.

"How was your weekend, Charles?" she asked.

"I went to visit my mother and father," he said.

"That sounds lovely," she replied with a smile, thinking that his tone of voice had made it sound anything but.

He gave her a quick frown before turning his gaze back to Laura's desk.

"I'm sure she'll be here soon," Susie said, walking over to the limescale-filled kettle in the corner and giving it a half-hearted rinse before filling it up and turning it on.

"I know that," Charles said, his cheeks flushing and his jaw tightening.

"It's nice when we're all here," Susie said, deciding to shift the focus, as though she'd just been looking forward to seeing the girl herself.

"Did you have a pleasant weekend?" Charles asked her, and she smiled at the fact that his high-handed manner couldn't quite hide the fact he was actually a nice lad underneath it all.

"I did, thanks. I got some of the supplies Sam suggested, and went for a picnic in Regent's Park." Susie could feel the smile spreading across her face at the memory of that, and of Dean giving her his office.

"Really?" Charles asked. "And you enjoyed that?"

"Oh, that sounds amazing," Laura's cheerful voice filled the room and Susie couldn't hold back the smile that grew as Charles looked Laura over, taking in her halter-neck top and short shorts, blushing a deep crimson. "A picnic in the park would be great in this weather." Laura fanned herself, grinning at them both.

"We could eat lunch in the square across from here one lunchtime?" Sam said, joining them, his usual rumpled trousers and T-shirt making him look nothing like the famous artist he was.

"Brilliant," Laura said, bouncing up and down on her toes and making her ringlets bounce with them.

As Charles's gaze was transfixed by the other parts of Laura that were bouncing along with her hair, Sam went up even further in Susie's estimation as she realised he was entirely oblivious to the lithe young body in front of him — despite the fact he was only in his late thirties, he was giving the nineteen-year-old a positively fatherly smile.

"Now that's settled," he said, "let's talk about approach to the work."

Susie listened intently as he talked about the importance of having a good work ethic.

"I know most people think being an artist, well, any kind of creative, is all about waiting for inspiration to hit."

"Like having a muse," Charles said.

"Exactly," Sam replied with a smile. "Unfortunately, waiting around for one of Zeus's daughters isn't going to make anyone a success. It takes regular, concerted effort and hard work."

Susie smiled; she knew all about hard work, and making the best of the little bits of free time she did have.

"Everyone has a different process and approach," he explained. "I can't promise you my approach is the right one, but I work every day."

"Surely it's a waste of time if you're not having a good day?" Laura asked.

"If I waited for good days, especially early on, I'd have almost never worked," Sam said with a laugh. "Even the days where you feel like everything you create is the sort of thing a three-year-old could do have their uses. You can learn a lot about what doesn't work for you, and use that knowledge to focus your efforts into the things that do work for you." He looked around, making sure he still had their full attention before continuing. "Look, if I'm having a day where nothing is coming together, I won't work as long, but I will still work for a few hours. If you want to make a career out of this, you have to treat it like a job, and that means having discipline about working on it. Every hour you work on your skill improves it, even when it doesn't feel like it's helping."

"But we all have uni, and I have a part-time job and stuff. What if I can't find time?" Laura asked, and Susie smiled.

"I know the answer to this one," she said, smiling at Sam, who nodded for her to go on.

"How much do you want it? Because if you want it enough, you have to work out what you can give up to make the time. I can't remember the last time I watched a soap on television, and I love them. I don't go to parties or clubs because I have to make choices with my spare time, and I choose this," she gestured around them.

At her words, she was surprised to realise that Charles looked determined, not what she would have expected from someone she suspected had been handed everything throughout his life. Laura's face was more what she'd expected. The girl looked crestfallen, in the way only someone so young could pull off. It was one of those moments in life when you realised that you couldn't have it all. Susie recognised the look, even though she'd been much, much younger when she'd realised life was all about trade-offs, no matter how much she wished it wasn't.

There was a small part of her that felt bad for bringing that stinging sense of reality to them, but she wouldn't have been doing them any favours by letting the 'have it all' myth continue. It was one of her biggest bugbears; you couldn't have it all, and if you did, you were simply driving yourself into the ground while giving off the kind of façade that only made other people feel inadequate.

"Not easy, but honest," Sam said. "When I started out, I was working twelve-hour shifts at a toilet roll factory and part-time at a pub."

"Two jobs?" Charles asked.

"The factory job paid the bills, the pub paid for my supplies," Sam said, giving them a grin. "I never thought I'd be living somewhere like this."

Susie was pleased to see Laura's shoulders square, as though realising just what those small sacrifices could achieve. Susie didn't harbour any illusions that her art would get her to a place where she could afford the sort of seven-figure property they were currently in, but if it let her help children tap into their creativity and pay the bills without having to take a second job, she'd be satisfied. If it gave her free time to create her own work as well, she'd be ecstatic.

Adding ink work to the charcoal image she'd been crafting of the pile of shattered glass Sam had placed in from of them, Susie glanced at the wall to her right. Sam had pinned up an array of images that seemed to hint at life and movement; they were unfinished and offered a visual record of how his current work was progressing. She looked back to her own work and frowned. She'd never be good enough.

"Breathe," Sam said, his voice close to her shoulder as he studied her work.

"Oh God," she breathed, her humiliation complete at him studying what was definitely not her best effort, not that her best effort could even remotely live up to Sam's work.

"You're too stiff," he said.

Susie instantly fixated on the tension in her shoulders, attempting to force her body to relax.

Gesturing for her to step aside, Sam moved into her place in front of the A1 sheet on her desk. "You have technical skill," he said, his hand following the lines she had just added to the image. "But…"

And here it came: she had no talent, she was never going to be good enough, he was going to kick her off the placement early. She tried to pull her thoughts back under control; she was twenty-eight, she didn't go into a panic spiral about things. So what if creating her own art, art that people would pay for, was the dream she never allowed herself to articulate? She'd been through tough things before; she could do it again.

"There's no passion here," Sam said. "You're holding yourself back. You need to flow with the work; even if it's bad, you need to feel something with every line you draw, every bit of colour you add. If you don't, no one else will."

Susie felt heat creeping across her cheeks. What was she doing here? She wasn't ever going to be good enough. "How do I do that?" she asked, swallowing her pride as she forced herself to remember why she was here: to learn, to be better.

Sam frowned and looked at his own partial work up on the walls. He was silent for a moment before replying. "You have to be prepared to let people see who you really are, let them feel what you feel."

She winced. She had been fourteen when her dad had stolen from their community, and left her and her mum behind without a second glance, and she'd worked hard to keep her feelings hidden ever since. She didn't know if she was capable of showing them now, of letting herself be that vulnerable.

CHAPTER FOURTEEN

Shoving her chair away from the kitchen table, Susie rubbed her hands over her face, hoping the action would stop the hot prickle in her eyes from building any further. She hadn't been able to face going into the study to do the real work she knew she should be doing, but working on a sketchpad wasn't going to help her make the changes she knew she had to make. Taking a deep breath, she closed her eyes; she wasn't going to give in to the despondency that had been building since Sam's words yesterday.

"Hey, what's up?" Dean asked, as he turned down the radio she'd been blasting in an effort to cheer herself up.

Of course, he had to walk in now, just when she was on the verge of falling apart.

"I didn't hear you come in," she said, deciding not to answer his question and clasping her hand to her chest in the hope he'd misread her reaction as shock rather than embarrassment at being caught about to have a meltdown. They'd been good friends in their youth, but it had never really been a 'talk about your feelings' kind of thing.

"Your work really is incredible," he said, when he finally dragged his gaze from her face and onto the image she'd been working on.

"It's not working," she said.

"What do you mean?"

"It's just not coming together properly." She knew it wasn't really an explanation, but how could she explain that instinctive sense that something intangible was missing? Something that would take the work from technically proficient to something that touched the soul, in a way that only art could do? She certainly wasn't about to tell him that she couldn't give her emotions to her efforts.

"It looks fantastic to me."

"Unfortunately, Sam doesn't agree," she said.

"Ahh."

Susie waited for the platitudes to follow, the ones everyone always resorted to, the 'art is subjective', 'you're better than anyone else we know' type of comments. The ones she knew were well meant, but only ever made her feel worse. It didn't matter if she was better than other people; that didn't bring her dream any closer, and it didn't get her the approval of someone she hugely admired.

"Maybe a change of perspective will help?" Dean asked.

"What do you mean?" she asked, her curiosity piqued at the idea Dean actually wanted to help in a practical way.

"Let's go out."

The idea appealed more than she wanted to admit. It didn't even matter where they went. Just the idea of getting away from the endless hours spent either at work or staring at her own subpar work was enough.

"But you have that programming thing to sort out," she said, reluctantly remembering that Dean had his own commitments.

"I do," he said, and her heart sank. "But I think it'd help me to take a break too."

He looked a little hopeful as he spoke, and she nodded her agreement. "Okay, let's skive off together," she said with a grin.

"I can't remember the last time I did something like this," Dean said, propping himself on one elbow as he took a bite of his Magnum and watched a cross-legged Susie twisting her cone to lick her melting ice cream. He'd suggested a trip out mostly because he couldn't bear the despondency he'd seen on Susie's face — and he'd have done anything to take that away — but he also realised that he needed more fun in his life.

"What, sat eating an ice cream on the South Bank?"

"Yes, that too, but I was thinking about when I'd last bunked off to have fun."

Susie laughed, a warm, genuine sound that Dean realised he'd missed over the last few years. "Me too," she said. "It was probably the last time we went into Bristol together."

The memory of the pair of them slipping away from Honeyford to visit the dodgy little club hidden away in a backstreet they'd found entirely by accident made Dean smile.

"It's a shame we couldn't get on the Eye," Susie said, disturbing his thoughts before they could follow that visit to the past too far.

"I know, but we'd have to be a lot more organised to get on it in peak tourist season."

"The woman said you had to book at least a few days ahead," Susie said. "Not like when we used to drive over to the fair in Bridgwater."

The annual travelling fair had been a huge hit, so much so that they'd driven the hour from Honeyford to visit it at least twice during its week-long run each year, spending far more than was sensible on the rickety rides and trying to win tat at the stalls. The opportunity for a bit of excitement had been too much to pass up, though.

"I suspect the view is a lot better on this one," Dean said, gesturing to the imposing metal and glass structure as it slowly turned, somehow looking as though it completely belonged despite the ancient stone of Westminster Bridge next to it. From their viewpoint, it seemed to tower over the entire city.

"You've never been on it?"

Dean shrugged. "Just one of those things you don't get around to doing when you live somewhere."

"I'd have loved to go on it," Susie said with a look on her face that made something inside of him regret that he hadn't been able to make it happen.

Dean's phone began to ring, and he pulled it from his shorts pocket. Seeing it was Grace made his heart sink just a little. "Sorry," he said, turning it so Susie could see the caller ID. "I'd better get this."

Susie just nodded and turned her attention to the Eye again. He didn't really want to answer, not wanting to risk the call casting a shadow over their day, but he knew if he didn't answer now, he'd only be forced to call Grace back later, and that would definitely erase any good feeling he might have at the end of the day.

"Hi, Mum," he said, not able to get any more in as she launched into chatter about his brothers and their respective partners and kids.

"Evie has been picked for a county football tournament this summer," she said, skipping the traditional greeting in her usual way as she shared her pleasure at her granddaughter's success.

"That's brilliant," Dean said. Even he couldn't feel churlish about his niece's achievement.

"And Joe has decided to try being a carpenter," she said, causing Dean to roll his eyes.

What a surprise, Joe had decided on yet another career to try. Leaning back until he was staring up at the blue sky, Dean focused on the wisps of cloud floating gently overhead.

"Nathan has said Joe can spend some time with him before he gets a job working for a carpentry firm, just so he can see if he really likes it," Grace continued. "That's nice of Nathan, isn't it?"

"Yes, great," Dean said. Bloody hell, how did Nathan turn Joe's flighty nature into something that Nathan himself could get brownie points for? The fact he had likely made the offer to Joe in an effort to get the lad to stop wasting employers' time was beside the point. It just made him look even more perfect in their parents' eyes.

"What about you?" Grace asked. "What are you up to?"

Dean glanced up to see Susie splitting her attention between her ice cream and the passing tourists. He licked his own, trying to stop the melting sweetness from dripping onto his hands. Well, he wasn't about to spoil his time with Susie by turning it into something for his parents to gossip over. He'd just about stopped seeing the accident at all when he looked at her, and he suspected mentioning her name would cause his mum to bring it up.

"I'm in with a chance of becoming a partner at work," he said, the words spilling out. Damn it, he'd wanted to wait and tell them when — if — he got the promotion, rather than building expectation now.

"Wow, that's amazing, Dean," Grace said. "They'd be so lucky to have you as a partner."

Despite himself he smiled at her words, and the confidence in them.

"So, when do they make the decision? Who else is in the running? Do you think you'll get it?"

And just like that the smile slipped; of course she couldn't just be pleased for him, she had to bring up all the questions that made it clear, to him at least, that she didn't think it was a sure thing he'd get it. He should have known she wouldn't think that; she knew he wasn't really good enough.

Tuning out, he gave the shortest answers he could to the rest of her questions, and when she finally took the hint and rang off, he gave a sigh.

Susie met his gaze, her expression puzzled, and he realised he should have done a better job of hiding the way the call had affected him, as now he was going to have to face another inquisition, and he definitely didn't want to explain any of this to Susie. How would he explain his own sense of inadequacy to a woman who, despite all the challenges life had thrown at her, held her head high and went for everything she wanted?

"Let's go and see the performers," she said, jumping to her feet as he silently thanked her for ignoring his change in mood.

"Sure, I'm done with this anyway," Dean said, moving towards the bin to dump the half-finished but suddenly unwanted ice cream.

"Hey," Susie called, arm extended, fingers curling in a 'come here' gesture. "Don't waste ice cream."

He laughed as she took it from him. "Still as sweet-toothed as ever."

She didn't answer him, just attacked the ice cream with a level of enthusiasm that belied the fact she'd literally just finished her own. The sight of her enjoying the treat he'd had his own mouth on moments before made him clear his throat. He led her off the crowded grass and onto the wide pavement that ran alongside the Thames. The water was calm but not still.

Small speedboats passed the larger river cruise boats, all packed with people enjoying the opportunity the wonderful weather was giving them to be out on the water.

Susie stopped at each of the street performers, taking the time to enjoy their work and throwing coins into the hats, cups, and guitar cases. She seemed particularly taken with the performers who covered themselves and their clothes in metallic paint and held a pose.

"She must be baking," Dean said, as they studied a woman dressed as a clown and painted entirely in gold. The heat was causing sweat to prickle his skin, even in just a short-sleeved shirt and tailored shorts.

"I'd love to know what they use," Susie said, not taking her eyes off the woman. "There isn't a single smudge, despite the heat. It's incredible."

The woman winked, making Dean jump, before she stepped off her box and doffed her hat at the small assembled group. She smiled and drank from a water bottle that had been in the box she'd stood on, before turning to Susie.

Dean tuned them out as he watched Susie and the gold woman chat about paint and make-up, simply enjoying the warmth of the summer, letting his memories of a similarly animated Susie wash over him. She'd always been such a contradiction. In the same year at school, they'd known each other their whole lives, but hadn't ever really hung out until their last couple of years at secondary school. He knew what had changed then; everyone did. After all, it wasn't often that someone's dad stole all the cash from the latest PFTA fundraiser and ran off, leaving his wife and daughter behind, but it had led to the most random rebellion he could have imagined. Dean knew he'd had a reputation for being a troublemaker back then. He'd never done anything criminal, or too dangerous, but was definitely the first one to instigate a prank or take a risk, so it hadn't been a surprise that a hurting good girl like Susie had sought him out. Together they'd caused all sorts of havoc, and through it all, she'd had the uncanny ability to talk to and connect with anyone. It was nice to see she still did.

"Well, that's my break over," the gold woman said. "I'd better get back to it."

"Can we get you a cold drink or anything?" Susie asked, as the woman climbed back onto her box.

"I'm all sorted. Thanks, though," she replied with a smile, gesturing to the box at her feet. "Have a great day." She shifted her limbs into a pose and froze.

As they made their way down the South Bank, Susie grabbed Dean's hand and pulled him towards the food stalls. The scents were rich and tempting despite the fact he'd not long eaten half an ice cream.

"We have to try something," Susie said, smile wide as she took a deep breath through her nose.

"You can't be hungry after eating all of your ice cream and most of mine."

"It was half of yours, and no, I'm not hungry, but are you seriously telling me you're not tempted to try something?"

"Come on then, we can share something," he said.

Slinging his arm around her shoulders, Dean steered them through the clusters of stalls, waiting for Susie to decide what she wanted, the scents of the array of foods stirring his appetite.

"How am I supposed to decide?" she asked, her head moving from the French stall selling duck in burgers to the chocolate being drizzled on fruit at the next one.

"Well, we can discount the deep-fried vegan pizza," Dean said, his nose wrinkling at the idea of something that should be dripping with dairy being vegan.

"Hey, don't knock vegan food until you've tried it," Susie said, turning towards him, her eyes glinting with amusement.

"Oh no," he said, "I know that look, and I don't like it."

Jostled by the milling crowds of people, she eased closer to him, her hand coming up onto his chest, and he found he couldn't take his eyes off the way her lips curled upwards.

"But you said I could choose whatever I wanted," she said, her eyebrows rising in challenge, and making it clear he wasn't going to be allowed to back out now.

"Dean," a sharp voice broke into his thoughts and he forced his eyes away from the plump curve of Susie's mouth.

"Amanda," Dean said, his stomach sinking at the sight of the woman who'd dumped him months ago. They'd lasted far longer than any of his other relationships, but they'd never quite connected in the way he knew she wanted. He'd finally thrown the last trace of her out of his flat, but he wasn't sure he was ready to face her, or the reality that it didn't matter how hard his partner was prepared to try, he didn't deserve a good relationship.

"What are you doing here?" she asked.

Dean opened his mouth to reply, not sure how he'd explain the fact he was here, with another woman, doing something she'd pleaded with him to do with her throughout their relationship, but Susie beat him to it.

"Hi," she said, easing away from him and sticking her hand out towards Amanda, her smile genuine and cheerful. "I'm Susie."

Dean knew he should be focused on the woman who'd approached them, but he found himself missing the feel of Susie's hand on his chest, the sensation of being pressed to her side.

Amanda looked at Susie's hand for a beat before finally shaking it. "You must be a better woman than I am," Amanda said. "I never managed to get him to do anything like this."

Susie turned to Dean; her brow furrowed in question. "I don't think that's a reflection on either of us," she said, her tone light.

"Don't you?" Amanda said, crossing her arms and staring at him, even though her words were addressed to Susie. "Well, don't expect too much from him. He isn't capable of a relationship."

Susie looked from Amanda to Dean and back again. Dean couldn't work out why Amanda was so worked up; they'd broken up nearly a year ago, and she'd dumped him. He was the one who'd been left hurting, not her.

"You broke up with me," he said, cursing the words for slipping out as he focused on avoiding Susie's gaze; he'd just admitted to being dumped and he didn't want to see her reaction to the fact he was so pathetic.

"You didn't really give me any choice," Amanda said. "I said the words, but you'd already all but ended it."

His jaw dropped; how had she rewritten the past so much?

"Forget it," she said. "I don't know why I came over. I should feel sorry for you; you'll never have a long-term relationship, and I'm happy dating again."

Dean felt himself flinch, but to his surprise, it wasn't that she was dating someone that caused it, it was her prediction for his future. He wanted more than that.

He found himself looking away from Amanda to Susie, unable to respond.

"How lovely," Susie said. "I hope he's good to you."

"He is," Amanda said. "Unlike Dean."

Dean felt rather than saw Susie stiffen next to him. There wasn't anything he could put his finger on, but he'd known her so well throughout their teenage years that he could sense the shift in her emotions.

"Well, I'm glad you've found someone who clearly makes you so happy," Susie said, her voice not fitting with the words. She paused for a beat before speaking again. "Just like Dean has made me."

As the words left her mouth, Dean stilled, not daring to say more as she slipped her arm around his waist, pressing her body to his side.

"It won't last," Amanda said, her eyes tracking Susie's movements.

"Oh dear, that would be unfortunate, given that we're getting married next month," Susie said.

Dean's head swivelled down to hers. There was a familiar glint in her eyes as she gazed at him, her hand on his chest.

"No engagement ring?" Amanda said, the words a half question, making Dean drag his eyes from Susie's back to his ex.

"It's getting cleaned. We want everything to be perfect for the big day. Don't we, darling?"

Dean found himself nodding.

"Oh, well, oh, good luck," Amanda said, turning and walking away, getting swallowed by the crowd in seconds.

"Okay, I want those," Susie said, pointing at a man carrying a cardboard box that looked like it was full of deep-fried shrimp, and completely ignoring the passive-aggressive conversation Amanda had started.

Trying to shake the odd feeling the last few minutes had left him with, Dean summoned a smile up from somewhere deep inside. He could have done without his inability to hold down a relationship being exposed to Susie, but her willingness to defend him filled him with a warmth that he wanted to hang on to.

"As long as it's not that vegan thing, I'm in."

CHAPTER FIFTEEN

Lifting her straw to her mouth with the exaggerated care of someone who had probably had too much to drink, Susie sucked up a mouthful of her vodka and coke, not taking her eyes off Dean.

"But she broke up with *me*," he said, frowning.

"Officially, but did you just do that thing men do where you behave so badly you gave her no choice?" Susie held his gaze as he thought about it for a minute, the process taking longer than it should have if he hadn't somehow been at fault.

"If you agree with her, why did you pretend we were getting married?" he finally asked.

Susie felt her cheeks warm. She hadn't expected him to sidestep the question, especially not by putting the focus onto her. If she was honest, there was a part of her — the part that remembered the girl who, despite her determination to avoid romance, had been just a little bit obsessed with the teenage version of Dean — that had liked the look of envy Amanda had given her. The fact Dean had gone along with the ruse had added a little something extra.

"No one gets to put you down like that," she said with a shrug.

Dean's eyes darkened as he watched her, as though measuring the sincerity of her words. "I don't think I behaved particularly badly," he said slowly, as though weighing his words. "But you heard her. I can't do relationships; they never last."

"Well, you obviously haven't met the right person," Susie said. "One day you will, and it'll all work out."

"It's nice that at least one of us is sure of that," Dean said, his head dipping down, a sense of melancholy washing over him.

"No, enough of that," Susie said, swatting his arm. "You brought me out for a day of fun, no getting all miserable on me!"

"Sorry," he said, lifting his head to meet her gaze. "You're right, fun it is, and it's my turn to buy the drinks."

"No, it's not. You bought the last round."

"Ah, but I got all gloomy, so I have to pay the miserable git tax and get them in." Dean gave her a wink as he stood and worked his way to the bar.

Susie's phone buzzed with a message as she watched Dean, his long frame leaning against the bar.

Bumped into your mum, she's doing great. Maggie x

Susie knew Maggie and Nathan had said they'd keep an eye on Dorothy, but getting the occasional update really helped put her mind at rest. Smiling, she tapped out a reply.

Thanks xx

Almost instantly, Maggie replied.

How's it going? What are you up to today?

Glancing up, Susie saw Dean working his way back to her.

Placement is great. Having a day out with Dean today, we went to see the Eye, getting sloshed in the pub now.

Thankfully, the fact it was a Wednesday afternoon meant that it wasn't too busy, and Dean quickly returned, placing a martini in front of Susie with a flourish. As soon as the glass was on the table, Susie's phone rang.

"Hi, Maggie," she said, picking it up with a grin on her face. "How are you and Nathan doing?"

"Never mind all that," Maggie said. "You got Dean Parker to go out, just for fun?"

Susie passed the phone to Dean, figuring he could speak for himself. After what was clearly a lot of good-natured ribbing, he rolled his eyes and hung up, passing the phone back to Susie.

"Honestly," he said. "Anyone would think I never have fun."

Susie laughed at the look of annoyance on his face. "What's with the martini?" she asked, gesturing to her glass.

"I thought you deserved a fancy drink as thanks for defending me today."

"You don't have to bribe me. I'll always have your back," she said, giving him a wink. "But I'll take it."

"I'm sorry," Dean said, his tone shifting to something more serious.

"You don't have to be sorry for bringing me a fancy drink," Susie said, winking again.

"I didn't mean that," he said.

"I know."

"I'm sorry for leaving," he said.

"We don't have to talk about this," she said, closing her eyes for a beat, as though that would make the conversation disappear along with her sight.

"I need to apologise," Dean said. "You were my best friend and I just left."

"Well, we're friends again now," Susie said, shifting in her seat. She didn't know why this was so hard; she was normally the first to call people out, but she really didn't want to have this conversation with Dean. She really didn't want him to know how long she'd blamed herself, or how much he'd hurt her. After half a dozen drinks, she knew it would all come spilling out if she let him pursue this conversation. "Apology accepted," she said. "Can we talk about something less depressing now?"

"What made you want to be an art teacher?" Dean asked, and she silently thanked him for not pushing it.

"Being creative has always helped me cope with things," Susie said. "I really like the idea of helping young people to find the same thing."

"That's really special," Dean said, stretching his arm across the table to place his hand on top of hers.

Eyes on their joined hands, she spoke again without thinking. "I just want to help people," she said, enjoying his warmth seeping into her. "I really want to be an artist in my own right as well, though." She pulled her hand back at the realisation of what she'd said, her head dropping to her lap. What had possessed her to share that bit of truth with Dean? She hadn't said those words out loud to anyone.

"And that's why Sam's criticism hurt so much," Dean said.

Susie's head snapped up to find him studying her carefully. She just nodded, the alcohol combining with her vulnerability to make it impossible for her to speak.

"Sometimes the things that hurt the most are the ones that push us to be better, but only if we're prepared to face the pain," Dean said quietly.

"That…" Susie said, the word barely audible. Clearing her throat, she started again. "That sounds like you're speaking from experience."

"I don't think I'd realised it, but I think I've been avoiding some things I should be working through," he said with a frown.

"Does this mean you have to pay the miserable git tax again?" Susie said, gesturing to her almost empty glass in an effort to change the subject before she admitted something she'd really regret sharing.

Dean gave her a knowing smile, making it clear he knew she was trying to change the subject again. "It does," he said, standing up and giving her the kind of cheeky grin that threw her right back to their youth, and the feelings she'd buried. "But for what it's worth, I think you should go for it. People would be lucky to be able to buy your art."

With that parting shot he headed to the bar, leaving Susie to fight a wave of desire for something with Dean that she was sure she'd long since stopped wanting.

CHAPTER SIXTEEN

Susie blinked at the sight of the man standing at the door to Dean's flat.

"Niall?" she asked, rubbing at the paint that had started to dry on the back of her hand.

"Hi," he replied. "It's Susie, isn't it?"

"Yes, but I'm afraid Dean isn't here," she said, wondering why Dean's friend-cum-nemesis had decided to turn up at his home.

"Oh no, I was really hoping to get his input on something," Niall said, running his hands through his hair in a way that was clearly designed to draw attention to the sort of locks that belonged on a poster advertising cologne.

"I don't know how long Dean will be," Susie said, resisting the urge to roll her eyes at his antics.

Leaning forward, he rested his forearm on the doorframe above her head and smiled. "I don't mind waiting."

Shrugging, she decided she'd better let him wait. She knew Dean was dealing with a lot at work and didn't want to add to his stresses by turning his colleague away.

Easing the door fully open, she gestured for Niall to come in. She indicated for him to sit, at which point she realised she couldn't exactly leave him on his own in Dean's home.

"I'm just going to grab a couple of bits. I'll be back in a sec," she said, not wanting to lose the momentum she'd developed before being interrupted. Heading to the office room that Dean had been letting her use as studio space, Susie grabbed a sketchpad and set of pencils. She couldn't continue with the paintwork, but she could work on the base sketches.

"Dean mentioned that you're an artist," Niall said.

Her chest seemed to swell at the words. Dean had said she was an artist — not studying to be an artist, not that she wanted to be an artist, but that she *was* an artist.

Susie nodded and looked down at her pad, her hands flying over the paper as she attempted to capture the intensity of the image that had popped into her mind fully formed, yet somehow intangible. Now she had to try to pin it to reality.

"Would it be okay if I got a drink?" Niall asked.

Susie glanced up, blinking hard, and realised she'd been completely ignoring him. "I'm sorry," she said. "I get lost in the process sometimes."

"It's no problem," Niall said, rising from the couch as if to go and help himself. Supressing a sigh, Susie realised that she'd have to go and get one for him. For all she knew, Dean had Niall around all the time and gave him the run of the place, but she didn't want Dean to think she'd been cavalier with his home.

"No, please sit, I'll get it. Would you prefer hot or cold?"

"Cold, a Coke if you have it?"

"No problem."

Holding the two cans, Susie dashed across the lounge to where she'd been sitting, and where Niall was now standing, her sketchpad in his hands. Seriously, who just picked up someone else's work and started looking through it uninvited?

"Um, here you go," she said, holding one of the cans out. As soon as he took the can, she could just take the sketchpad from him. She hated people looking at her work before it was finished and while she didn't want to offend him, she would if it meant getting him to put her pad down.

"You're very talented," he said, holding the pad out to her and saving her from her dilemma.

Susie took it gratefully, sinking back into the couch, fully expecting Niall to take the hint and go back to the other couch with his drink.

Instead he sat next to her, so close she could feel the heat from his body radiating into hers. "I particularly like what you've done here," he said, pointing to the part of the image she was the most unhappy with.

"Thanks," she said, turning to face him.

"I'm not surprised someone so beautiful is able to create such incredible work," he said, his hand reaching up and his palm curling around her cheek.

Susie suppressed a sigh; this was where being polite got you. Did he really think that sort of shallow statement was a compliment? She raised her own hand, intending to ease his away from her face.

"Sorry to interrupt." Dean's voice seemed to echo through the room.

Her head swung to meet Dean's gaze as she jumped to her feet. "Niall was just waiting for you," she said, mentally slapping herself. Why was she acting like she needed to justify or explain anything?

"I see," Dean said, something flashing across his features so fast she couldn't pinpoint it before he turned to Niall. "What can I help you with?"

"I was working through the user experience and wanted to discuss an idea with you," Niall said, giving a half smile as he rested his hand on Susie's arm. "Susie's been keeping me company while I waited."

At the movement, Dean's features shuttered, the tension Susie was used to seeing in them hidden by an alien blankness.

"Really?" she said to Niall, raising her eyebrows. If he thought he could use her to wind Dean up, he had another think coming.

"What? Well, you were," Niall stuttered, obviously not used to being called out on his behaviour.

"You know what your tone was implying," Susie said, taking the opportunity to pick up her pad and step further away from Niall.

"I'm glad you're back," she said, focusing on Dean and giving him a warm smile before taking the opportunity to escape. She didn't mind calling Niall out, but she wasn't going to let it escalate either. That would only hurt Dean.

CHAPTER SEVENTEEN

"Something's changed," Sam said, studying Susie's work.

Susie held herself still, and she'd have held her breath if he hadn't been taking so long over his inspection of her latest attempt. Was he actually going to give her a compliment? She'd asked Sam if she could use his workshop this evening, needing to get out of Dean's flat while Niall was still hanging around.

He turned his intense gaze to meet hers. "There is more feeling here," he said, and her spirits soared, until he added, "but you're still holding back."

Susie flinched, knowing what Sam was saying was true, but also knowing she'd exposed more of her heart in this image than she'd ever done before. The fact it still wasn't enough just made her feel as if she'd never achieve anything like the quality of work she wanted to be able to produce.

"Right," Sam said, "let's have a drink."

Susie blinked hard. "What?" she asked, confused by the sudden change of subject.

"This isn't working this evening, for either of us," he said. "Let's get drunk and enjoy the last of the sunshine."

Susie glanced at the huge sheet Sam had been working on and sighed. If that was his idea of it not working, she had no chance.

Stretching out on the wooden loungers that were positioned neatly on Sam's patio, Susie accepted a glass of lager and let herself relax. He was right, she wasn't going to get anything achieved this evening, and Charles and Laura had long since left, planning a night of clubbing.

"Sorry," a voice said, breaking into her thoughts. "I didn't realise Sam had company."

"Michael," Sam's voice called. "This is Susie; she's here on the study placement."

"Oh," Michael said, watching Susie with a level of interest she wasn't used to.

"Have you brought my order?" Sam said, pulling Michael's eyes from her.

As the two talked, Susie took the opportunity to study the new arrival. Wearing torn jeans and an eighties band T-shirt, he had hair that was loose around his shoulders, his nose was pierced and his ears sported claw stretchers. Slender and of average height, he looked good, like someone thoroughly comfortable in his own skin.

After Michael had carried the food through to Sam's kitchen, Sam joined him. Susie let herself enjoy the warmth of the evening, closing her eyes as she stretched out on the lounger.

"I think you might have an admirer," Sam said.

Susie gave him a wry smile. "I don't really date," she said with a shrug.

"Why not?"

"I don't have much luck," she said, slipping her sunglasses on to avoid meeting his gaze. "The men I fancy tend to be pretty unreliable."

"I'm sure you'll find the right person one day," Sam said with a smile as he topped up her glass.

"We can't all end up with adoring supermodels," Susie said, referencing the fact that Sam and his girlfriend of the last couple of years were regularly plastered across the tabloids.

"True," he said with a smile as he leant back into his own lounger. "So, what has you so guarded, then?" Sam asked, making Susie choke on the mouthful of drink.

"What? Nothing. I'm not guarded," she spluttered.

Sam raised his eyebrows. "No, clearly not," he said with a laugh. "You just hold your feelings back for no reason."

"Damn artist being all observant," she said, trying to keep the mood light.

"Look, you don't have to tell me anything," he said, holding her gaze. "But you need to be honest with yourself. If you want to achieve the sort of work I know you're capable of, you have to let yourself be vulnerable."

Susie turned away, studying the slight wisp of cloud that was gently moving across the otherwise blue sky. The silence was so deep that she could have convinced herself they were in the countryside, rather than the centre of one of the world's busiest cities. "My dad did something awful when I was younger, and I've had to try to live that down ever since," she finally said, the words thick and hard to say. She didn't know what had possessed her to admit that, but there was something about Sam's direct and self-assured manner that made her feel a level of comfort she hadn't felt with anyone in a long time.

"He didn't...?" Sam started, as though not sure how to phrase his question.

Susie glanced at his face and realised he was imagining some kind of dreadful abuse. "No, God no," she said, shaking her head firmly; he'd been self-centred and feckless, but thank goodness she'd never had to experience that sort of trauma. "He stole the money the PFTA had been fundraising for a new mobile classroom."

Somehow, the fact he'd imagined something so much worse had made it easier for her to tell him the truth. She'd never actually told anyone; everyone around them at the time knew, and they always made sure to tell anyone else who moved to the area. The only other people she knew were from her university course, and she certainly hadn't been about to tell them that her father had preferred money to her and her mother. It was funny, though; she realised that saying the words out loud at last made the whole thing sound ridiculous.

"You're from a small village?" Sam asked.

Susie nodded.

"Damn, that must have been hard," he said, taking a swig from his own glass.

The fact that he clearly understood the challenge of dealing with gossip, speculation and the endless snide remarks eased something inside her.

"That sounds like the voice of experience," she said, shifting so she could study Sam more clearly.

He nodded, his face twisting with a wry expression. "Coming from a traditional Yorkshire village and wanting to be an artist don't go together very well."

"Well, you've certainly proved you were right to ignore any criticism," Susie said, lifting her glass to him.

"Aye, that I have," he said, giving her a grin.

"So, what made you move to London?" she asked.

"I needed a change of scenery," he said.

"Sounds like there's a story there?"

"Let's just say that when the novelty of dating the local bohemian wore off, I was summarily dropped."

"Ah, a broken heart," Susie said.

Sam just shrugged, clearly not wanting to expand.

"And now you're dating a supermodel," she said, giving him a grin.

"And now I'm dating a model," he said, raising his glass in salute. "Although, Marina would love being called a supermodel."

"Shall I get us a top-up?" Susie asked, determined to change the subject. She knew all about being left behind. Sam had clearly moved on, and she wasn't going to poke a wound that felt all too familiar.

CHAPTER EIGHTEEN

"Aren't you going on a date later?" Susie said, putting the takeaway cups into a cardboard carrier so Dean would be able to manage the half dozen coffees he'd ordered. The routine of seeing him during her shifts at Ground Up was something she was starting to enjoy a little too much.

"Ah, it didn't really work out with Lydia," he said, rubbing the back of his head in a way that had her wondering just what the texture of his shorn hair would feel like, as he awkwardly studied the counter between them.

"Oh, but she seemed lovely."

"She was," he said with a shrug.

Sensing that he didn't really want to talk about it, and not really wanting to discuss another woman, Susie didn't push the conversation.

"So, do you think your art colleagues would like to come for dinner, then?" Dean asked, repeating the offer to have them round for the evening.

"I don't know," Susie said honestly. "But I could ask them. It would be really great to hang out with them socially. Are you sure you don't mind, though?"

"No, it'll be nice to meet the people you talk about so much. I thought I'd invite a couple of people from work as well so everyone can mix."

"You know Sam won't bring Marina, don't you?" she said, giving him a wink. "She's on a shoot somewhere, maybe Ibiza, I think."

"I'm not suggesting it so I can meet Marina," Dean said, rolling his eyes good-naturedly.

"Okay, it sounds great, thanks. I'll message them. So, can I tempt you with something delicious for dessert?" Susie asked, gesturing to the display cabinet that was full of Momin's creations.

Dean eyed her, his cheeks turning a gentle pink before his gaze moved away to the pastries. "Yes, good idea, what do you recommend?"

"I don't think I could choose just one. I've tried just about all of them now, and every single one is amazing."

"Now, that's what I like to hear," Momin said, coming up behind Susie and giving Dean a grin. "She's good at upselling, this one."

Dean returned his smile. "She could always talk me into just about anything when we were growing up," Dean said, making Susie roll her eyes. She still felt the slight sting of worry that he was having a dig at her for making him go out that night, but had spent enough time over the years convincing herself she wasn't responsible that it was like a muted zing rather than the intense pain she'd had initially.

"Like it ever took much persuading," she said with a laugh.

"Well, your presence here has certainly increased the amount of business we get from upstairs," Momin said, referring to the tech company that Dean worked for that took up all of the upper floors of the building they shared.

Susie looked from Momin to Dean, her brow furrowed in question, only for the pink of Dean's cheeks to deepen.

The idea that Dean was making the trip to buy the daily coffees just because of her presence warmed her. Perhaps they could find their way back to their old friendship after all.

That evening, Susie joined Dean in welcoming each of the guests as they had arrived. It had given her a surprisingly domestic feeling. Somehow, she'd made it to almost thirty without ever having had a house party. When she thought about having one at the home she shared with Dorothy, she snorted. Ignoring all the tidying that would be necessary to clear the amount of stuff her mum hoarded, she'd then have to deal with the bulk of local people only showing up to nosy around the Lucas house so they could gossip about the family even more.

It was a unique experience to be with people who didn't have any idea about that part of her life — well, apart from Dean, but he'd proved years ago that he saw her entirely separately from that incident. If only he could see her separately from the accident, their friendship might just stand a chance.

"So, how long have you and Dean been friends?" Laura asked, perching on the arm of Charles's chair in a way that had the lad grinning broadly. Logically, Susie knew there was at most eight years between her and the other two, but for her, those eight years were filled with a kind of growing up that you only did in the most painful way possible. It made the gap between them seem like the kind of canyon she'd normally be more than capable of traversing, but after a few drinks, and the level of excitement that Laura exhibited for everything and everyone, she was tired, and feeling every day of those years.

She gestured to Dean for him to take on the mantle.

"We've known each other since we were little," Dean said. "Susie's family moved to Honeyford, that's the village I was born in, when we were about seven."

"My mum was from there. She'd moved away when she married my dad, but she got homesick so they moved back together," Susie said. She hadn't told anyone this for years;

everyone she knew already knew every painful detail of her life. Telling the tale now, she was surprised to realise she'd mentioned her dad, something she avoided at all costs because that inevitably led down a road to questions she didn't want to answer and tales she didn't want to tell. Her words made her wonder just what it was about Honeyford that Dorothy had felt homesick for, because as far as Susie could tell, all the place seemed to have to offer was an endless amount of judgement.

Damn it, she was getting maudlin and bitter. Pasting a smile on her face, she realised Dean was talking about their past.

"We didn't really get to know each other properly until we were about fifteen," he said.

"Oooh, and just how well did you get to know each other?" Laura asked with a look on her face that made it clear exactly what she was really asking.

Dean met Susie's gaze before rolling his eyes and giving her a wink. "Not *that* well," Dean said, turning to give Laura a wry look.

"I can't believe you've been friends for all these years, and nothing has happened between you," Laura said, clearly unconvinced by Dean's words.

Susie froze, and if it hadn't been for the fact her attention had been completely on Dean, she'd have missed his almost imperceptible flinch at Laura's statement. She knew it wasn't because he thought people might believe they'd slept together.

A little part of her might have been tempted to let the discussion continue, even to redirect it so that Dean was backed into giving some sort of answer, any kind of answer, because whatever he said would tell her something, and surely something was better than the emptiness she was facing right now.

Catching Sam watching her with a look in his eye that made her realise he was probably the only person in the room, besides her and Dean, that was picking up on the subtext, decided for her. She wasn't about to air her dirty laundry in front of a man she respected and wanted to impress.

"What about you, Laura?" Susie asked, determined to derail the conversation. She wanted Dean to explain about the seven-year gap in their friendship, but not enough to hear it in front of an audience, and if either of them admitted to the gap, there would be no avoiding the answer. She briefly wondered whether her concern was about hearing the truth, or fear that he'd somehow dismiss the importance of leaving her behind.

"What about me?" Laura asked, her enormous eyes widening further.

"Do you have someone special waiting for you at home?" Susie asked, half watching Charles as he tensed, waiting for the answer.

"No," Laura said, shaking her head so her ringlets bounced in a way that just seemed to add to her air of innocence. Turning to Charles, she blushed a deep red before speaking again. "No one."

Susie was sure that Charles would be mortified to realise how obvious the smile was that spread across his cheeks at Laura's words, but she felt her own smile grow at the burgeoning relationship. With Laura's working-class background and enthusiasm for life contrasting Charles's stiff, uncertain approach to people around him, but deep ambition, they would be good for each other. Even if nothing came of their relationship at the end of this placement, they would both always have the memory of a special summer that helped them both see the world from a different perspective.

Meeting Sam's gaze, Susie smiled at the wink he gave her; his thoughts were clearly heading in the same direction as her own.

"Alex," Susie said, turning her attention to Dean's colleague who she hadn't yet spoken to after their initial greetings. "How long have you worked at Social Software?"

"A few years," he said, with a shrug that made his curtain of dark hair fall over his eye. "I started just after Dean, but I'm just the receptionist."

"It's nice to have a stable job," Susie said, giving him an encouraging smile. "People always underestimate receptionist jobs. If it wasn't for the receptionist, most places would descend into chaos within days."

Her words seemed to warm him, and he finally pushed his hair back from his face, giving her a soft smile. "Most people think it's boring," he said with another shrug.

"Well, I work in a bar and a coffee shop at the moment, but when I'm at home I work at a pub and as an administrator slash receptionist for a local accountancy firm, so I get how challenging it can be."

Alex leant a little closer. "People seem to forget we know all their secrets," he said with a smile, lifting one eyebrow to punctuate his point.

Susie laughed, the sound bursting from her. It wasn't what he'd said so much as the realisation that this seemingly shy and meek man had a sense of humour that veered just the right side of mischievous.

"Please tell me you know some about Dean?" she asked, leaning a little closer as though bringing him into her confidence, but turning to give Dean a cheeky wink as she did so.

She was surprised to find him studying her with a slight frown, but shook it off as concern that Alex would tell her something embarrassing. Or worse, that she'd share a childhood tale with Alex. She wouldn't, but Dean didn't really know her well enough anymore to be sure of that.

Instantly, her mood dropped. She was foolish to think she and Dean could be friends again. Whatever she did, friendship was a two-way street, and despite the fact he'd suggested this evening, she wasn't really sure what Dean wanted. She had a horrible suspicion he didn't know either.

CHAPTER NINETEEN

Heading through the underground car park towards her car so she could get across the city to Sam's with her finished canvas, a dash of movement made Susie pause. She'd grown up in the countryside, so she wasn't unused to seeing rats, but there was something about the shaded figure under her car that made her hesitate. Edging closer, she bent to the side, trying to get a better angle.

"What are you doing?" Dean's voice broke the silence.

Jumping, Susie raised her free hand to her chest. "There's something under there," she said, gesturing to her car. "What are you doing up so early?"

"I'm going for a run," Dean said, gesturing to the designer trainers he was wearing as he popped one earbud out.

Her eyes landed on the jogging pants that seemed to highlight every muscle in his solid thighs without clinging to them in the slightest, before she forced her gaze away. Despite the fact Dean had arranged a nice evening earlier in the week, it was clear that the friendship she thought they'd been rebuilding wasn't going to work. They had too much history to overcome. She'd hoped to be up and gone before he was awake this morning, the same as she'd done for the last few days. Admiring his thighs hadn't been on the agenda.

"Is it a rat?" he asked.

"No, I don't think so," Susie said, bending again.

As she eased closer, she heard a startled meow and saw a small ball of dark fur shoot forward, but instead of appearing in front of the car, it seemed to vanish.

"Well, at least we know it's a kitten," Dean said.

"Yes, but where did it go?" Susie asked, glancing around.

"I have a horrible feeling it's in your car," he replied. "Why don't you pop the bonnet and we'll check."

"But I have to get to Sam's to meet him and the others," Susie said. "I don't have time to have a kitten in my car."

"Well, maybe it just went to the side. Let's check before you start the engine, though," Dean said.

Opening the door, Susie pulled the lever to release the lock on the bonnet, and by the time she'd walked back to the front of the vehicle, Dean had already propped it open and was bending over, looking into the mass of stuff that Susie couldn't identify with the torch light on his phone.

"It's official, you have a squatter." He gestured with the light to one corner, where the fur was barely visible between bits of metal.

"How are we going to get it out? I can't be late."

Dean reached forward but couldn't fit his hand between the engine parts. Susie tried, but even her smaller hand couldn't get close to the kitten, although that didn't stop it appearing to burrow a little further into the vehicle.

"Let's try to tempt it out," Dean said. "I'll be back in a minute."

Susie kept her attention on the small patch of fur that was visible, and waited. When Dean returned, she turned to face him. "If I hadn't seen her run, I could have killed her by starting the car," she said, feeling a little wobbly at the thought.

"But you didn't," he said, resting his hand on her shoulder. She resisted the urge to lean into him, grateful that he hadn't tried to pretend it would have been fine, or dismiss her fears.

"Now then, let's see if any of this works," Dean said, opening the carrier bag he had in his hands.

He lifted a tin of tuna out of the bag and, using the ring pull, took the top off and scraped the contents onto a plate.

"Let's put it close enough for her to smell," Susie said, placing the plate to the side of the vehicle and moving back.

"This might take a while," Dean said, sitting down, his back to the concrete wall so he could keep an eye on the car.

"You could go for your run; we don't both need to wait here," Susie said.

"What, and miss the excitement?" he asked, patting the ground next to him for her to join him. "Alex has been asking about you," Dean continued, eventually speaking into the silence that Susie hadn't felt capable of breaking.

"He has?" she asked, not really bothered either way, but so relieved that Dean had spoken that she didn't want to risk him falling silent again.

Dean nodded, his eyes fixed firmly on the food they had left for the kitten.

"I think he wants to ask you out," Dean said, his tone even.

"Oh, well, he seems nice enough," Susie said.

"Do you want to go out with him?"

"Maybe?"

"Well, you do or you don't, it's not that hard," Dean said, sounding slightly annoyed.

"Has he asked you to ask me?" Susie said, turning to face Dean fully.

"No," Dean said, still refusing to turn and meet her gaze.

Rolling her eyes, Susie sighed, her estimation of Alex going up by a notch; at least he wasn't resorting to primary school tactics.

"Well, how about I worry about it if he asks me?" she said, turning away from Dean and studying the plate as well. He shouldn't have started a conversation he didn't want to have. Besides, it was none of his business who she dated.

A small *meep* sounded from the direction of her car and Susie found herself leaning forward. Finally, another *meep* and then the small ball of fur appeared, black except for a pale stripe that appeared to run right around its stomach, and so tiny the creature would fit into the palm of her hand. She sat motionless, willing the animal to eat some of the tuna, so hopefully they could get close enough to catch it while it was eating. The poor thing was only going to get hurt if they left it roaming the underground car park.

It sniffed at the dish suspiciously before burying its face in the meal. Before Susie could move, Dean had shot across the short distance and grabbed the kitten, gently lifting it with one hand as he seized the plate of tuna with the other. The kitten began to mewl pitifully until Dean brought the fish within its reach, at which point it began to happily stuff itself again.

"Hello, sweetie," Susie said, gently stroking the kitten's head, as the small creature seemed to arch into her palm, welcoming the attention. "You are just perfect," she said softly. She'd never even considered getting a pet; her life had been too full for too many years to want to be responsible for another life, but in that moment, she completely understood why people had pets. Maybe she could consider getting a cat when she went back home. Surely they couldn't be too much work.

"Well, it doesn't feel underfed," Dean said, giving her a smile. "I wonder if it belongs to someone in the building."

"Maybe," Susie said. "What can we do with it until we find its owner?"

"I'll take it up to the flat. You head over to Sam's with all your stuff. I'll put a note on the resident's noticeboard and see if anyone claims her."

Susie continued stroking the kitten, finding herself strangely reluctant to walk away.

"Susie, you're going to be late," Dean said softly.

She looked up to meet his gaze and found herself swallowing at the gentleness she found in his expression. She looked back at the kitten.

"I'll make sure no one takes her before you're home again," he said.

Susie gave the kitten one more stroke before stepping back.

Climbing into her car, Susie turned the key and the engine kicked to life. Turning to wave her goodbyes to Dean, she sucked in a breath, knowing the sight of him gently cradling the kitten to his chest would stay with her for far longer than was healthy for her heart.

CHAPTER TWENTY

Dean watched Liquorice race up to Susie the minute she opened her bedroom door. She was wearing her habitual jeans and trainers, but it was the T-shirt that drew his attention as she bent down to pick up the kitten that he seemed to have adopted and named.

"No one has claimed her yet, then?" Susie asked, holding the kitten in the crook of her arm and stroking it.

"No," Dean said with a shrug. "It's only been a few days, though." He said it as though he was still half expecting someone to claim ownership, when the reality was that he knew if anyone in the building owned the creature, they'd have seen the sign he'd put up next to the residents' post-boxes on the ground floor by now.

"I hope we can keep you," Susie said, cooing to Liquorice.

"And then you'll leave me with a pet when you head back to Honeyford?" Dean said, regretting the words as soon as he spoke them, because of the way Susie's expression dropped.

"Sorry, I hadn't thought that far ahead. I could take her with me, though?" she suggested.

"Let's worry about it if no one claims her," he said. "You look nice," he added, unable to stop the words from slipping out. Susie's T-shirt was plain purple but was doing something that seemed to emphasise her slender figure in a way that was sexier than the most revealing dress any of his recent dates had worn. How was a T-shirt sexy?

"Thanks," she muttered, her cheeks reddening at the compliment.

"So where are you going?"

"Just for pizza," she said with a shrug. "Alex suggested it."

"A date with food, sounds like your perfect kind of night," Dean said, his chest tightening. He liked Alex; the guy was nice — a little younger than he'd have thought Susie would go for, but a decent enough guy, if not too straight-laced and boring for Susie. She should be dating someone who challenged her and made her laugh.

His thoughts went back to the evening he'd spent with Susie's friends and some of his colleagues. He'd thought a house party with other people would help Susie to feel more settled here; he found he loved having her around, and the memories of the accident were coming less frequently now. If he'd realised the night would give Alex the courage to approach Susie a couple of days later while she was working at Ground Up to ask her out, he'd have thought twice about it. He scowled at the realisation he'd brought this on himself. It definitely wasn't that he minded Susie dating; he just didn't see her with someone like Alex.

"You're right," she said with a laugh, and he realised she was responding to his food comment. "Damn, I need to make sure all my dates take me for food in the future."

"How many dates are you planning to go on?" Dean asked, feeling his scowl deepen.

"As many as I like," Susie said, closing the distance between them with a smile that seemed to promise all kinds of mischief.

Dean waited to see what she would do, unable to take his eyes from hers. Her eyes dropped to his mouth and he took a deep breath, absorbing the rich floral scent of her perfume. The last time he'd been so close to her, she'd been wearing the same scent. How could he remember that? The images that filled his mind, of her stretched out in a hospital bed, superimposed over the reality of her standing in front of him.

Guilt hit him with the force of a wave, forcing him to take a step back, his chest tightening.

Her features seemed to close off from him, and she thrust her arms out towards him. Blinking hard, Dean looked down to see she was holding out Liquorice for him to take. Without instruction from his brain, he took the bundle, and watched Susie turn away from him, grabbing her bag she walked towards the door.

"Don't wait up," she called back, the words lilting and happy.

"Well, that went well," Dean said to Liquorice, who wriggled to be put down.

How had he remembered the scent of Susie's perfume? She'd always worn so little of it that you had to stand really close to her to get the slightest hint of it, despite the richness of the scent. He remembered that night in almost excruciating detail; now the scent of Susie at his side was added to the memory he could torture himself with. Liquorice twisted again and he gave up, crouching to set her down.

"Great, another woman who doesn't want to be around me," he said as she darted away, running to the door, as if wanting to follow Susie out into the night.

CHAPTER TWENTY-ONE

Dean hadn't seen Susie since her date with Alex a few days ago; in fact, he'd very deliberately tried to schedule himself around her endless shifts, so he didn't have to face her. It had been bad enough witnessing the way Alex had almost skipped through his days at work. He didn't need to see Susie doing the same thing. The fact Niall had been just as hacked off that Alex had succeeded where he'd failed didn't help.

Slipping his shoes off, Dean pushed them into their space on his shoe rack. He'd had an awful day and he just wanted to drink until he forgot it. It was bad enough dealing with the sight of Susie. Surely you shouldn't be attracted to someone at the same time as being unable to look at them without seeing them laid out on a hospital bed, or worse, trapped in a car next to you, a car that you'd been driving. Now he had to put up with the fact Niall was closer than him to solving the coding issue, and on top of that, he'd been sent home with a flea in his ear for getting short-tempered with Alex.

Sure, the guy had only been trying to make arrangements for the meeting with the investors, but did he have to be so bloody chipper while he was doing it?

Walking out to the kitchen, Dean decided he couldn't be bothered to eat; he was just going to drink away the rare evening at home, and hopefully fall unconscious early enough to have more than the few hours a night he'd been managing lately.

He frowned at the sight of Susie standing at the sink, drinking a long glass of water. "Where are you going?" he asked, realising she had her shoes on. It was too late for her to be starting a work shift, and she was wearing the dress she'd worn to the retirement party.

"I'm meeting Alex," she said, bending to place the glass in the dishwasher.

"You're seriously going on another date with Alex?" Dean asked, staring at her with an incredulous expression on his face.

"Yes, why not?"

"Why not?" he said, knowing his tone was ugly.

"Are you just going to repeat everything I say?" Susie asked, hands on her slim hips, drawing his gaze down her petite frame.

"Are you really telling me you like Alex?"

"Why wouldn't I?" Susie said, frowning at him. "He's pleasant enough."

"Can you hear yourself?" Dean said. A voice inside of him told him he should just shut up, but he found he didn't want to. The Susie he'd grown up with wouldn't have settled for 'pleasant enough', and the grown-up Susie definitely deserved more than that.

She leant against the kitchen wall and gestured for him to continue. The movement was tightly controlled in a way that suggested he would be better off just shutting up, but he found he couldn't stop himself.

"Pleasant enough?" he asked. "That's good enough for you, is it?"

"Why shouldn't it be?" she asked.

"Why?" He stepped further into the kitchen. "Susie, you are fun and mischievous and passionate; you need someone who challenges you, who encourages you to be everything you are capable of being. You shouldn't settle for pleasant."

"Well, maybe I like pleasant; maybe I like the fact that it comes with dependable."

"Dependable?" Dean laughed, aware it was a harsh, brittle sound. "You're so busy trying to prove to everyone you're reliable, that you're not your dad, that you've lost sight of who you are and what makes you happy."

Susie flinched as though he'd slapped her, and the voice in his head that had been gently suggesting he shut up shifted gear, screaming at him to apologise, but he wasn't going to. She needed to hear this, and he needed to say it.

"Like you'd know anything about that," Susie said, sniping back at him. "Do you even know what you want, or are you simply determined to avoid anyone and anything that might make you happy?"

It was Dean's turn to flinch. He didn't avoid happiness. He just couldn't seem to find anyone who wanted him for him. Deciding he wasn't about to let her off the hook that quickly, he pulled the conversation back. "You know I'm right. The Susie I knew would have been having fun, taking chances and fairly sure that no one was worth her time dating. Now you're so busy trying to prove you're better than your dad, you don't seem like yourself anymore. When was the last time you did something you know you shouldn't have done?" he asked, the words a challenge as he held her gaze. Her cheeks flushed, her jaw tightening.

"How dare you?" Susie spat the words at him. "How dare you bring him up. How dare you act as though you know me, or know anything about me?"

"I know you, Susie. I know what makes you tick, and dating someone like Alex isn't you. He's boring."

She raised an eyebrow at him, a calmness seeming to descend over her features that made him realise he'd very definitely gone too far. "You used to know me, you knew every part of me that mattered, but the day you left me alone in that hospital, you gave up any right to any opinion of me. You were the centre of my world, but you abandoned me when I needed you the most." Her voice cracked on the last of her words and her gaze dropped to the floor, but not before he saw the tears glistening there.

He'd made her cry. He'd already felt terrible, but it turned out he could indeed feel worse. He'd never considered that she'd feel abandoned. He'd been so wrapped up in his own guilt, so certain that she'd never forgive him, that he'd run before he had to face her rejection. He'd never considered that he could be wrong. Taking a step towards her, he reached out, wanting to wrap his arms around her and explain. Well, he wasn't sure he'd ever be able to explain, but he needed to do something, anything to ease her pain.

"No," Susie said. Her voice was strong and clear as she lifted her hand, placing her palm on his chest.

Meeting her gaze, Dean was surprised to see the strength and determination in her eyes, despite the tears that still tracked down her cheeks.

"You don't get to do this," she said, before she side-stepped him and walked out of the door.

CHAPTER TWENTY-TWO

Susie watched Alex, listening to yet another tale of courier delivery mix-ups. She'd pulled herself together by the time she'd arrived at the restaurant, not wanting Alex to realise she'd been upset. This one was fancier than the pizza place they'd been to for their first date, but as she tugged on the hemline of the dress she'd felt so elegant in at Dean's side, she realised she preferred the relaxed atmosphere of the first place.

Gulping her glass of wine, she realised she'd have to stop drinking if she didn't want all of her whirling thoughts to fall out.

"And then I had to run two blocks to catch up with her, just so I could tell her she had her skirt tucked into her knickers," Alex said, the words coming out with the kind of perfect cadence that only came with a frequently told tale.

Giving him a smile and forcing a chuckle, Susie turned her eyes back to the menu. Dean's words kept rolling around her head. When *was* the last time she'd done something she knew she shouldn't have? She'd never been really wild, but she'd known how to cut loose and enjoy herself. All she did now was work, and when she did date, they were pleasant guys who didn't light a fire under her. She even made sure they'd been on at least a dozen dates before she deigned to have boring sex with them. Was Dean right? Was she so worried about making sure people knew she wasn't like her dad that she'd stopped living?

"Are you okay?" Alex asked her, drawing her out of her self-pitying thoughts. The genuine concern in his expression made her smile.

"I'm fine," Susie said. "Sorry if I'm not great company tonight, it's been a long few days."

"You're always good company," Alex said, giving her a shy smile.

She tilted her head, studying the man opposite her. At just a couple of inches taller than her, he wasn't particularly tall for a man, but he was beautifully proportioned. His slim hips and chest gave him the sort of look that was more suited to an artist than Sam's broad, tall stature. His long fingers played with the stem of his wine glass, as though her in-depth attention made him nervous.

"Why don't we go back to your place?" Susie suggested.

"We haven't even ordered our main course yet," Alex said with a small frown.

She just held his gaze and raised her eyebrows. The moment her meaning became clear to him was obvious. He flushed and began to fidget.

"Oh, um, yes, that sounds like a great plan," he said, a smile growing on his face and his eyes lighting up. "Let me just pay for our drinks and starters and we can go."

There, she was doing something crazy and unplanned. Dean could take his opinion and shove it.

Alex's studio apartment was the kind of property Susie expected most people who lived in London had to make do with. The combined bedroom and living area was small but well-formed and, other than the clothes that were strewn on his bed, the place was tidy. She smiled at the thought of him changing his outfit multiple times in an attempt to find the right one for their date. She liked the idea of him making an effort to impress her.

"Just let me tidy these away," he said, his pale cheeks flushing.

"Don't worry," Susie said. "Do you have anything we can drink?"

"Yes, yes, of course," Alex said, heading towards the corner that was clearly the kitchen. "Would wine be okay?"

"Perfect."

Once Alex handed her a glass of wine, Susie took a sip before placing it on the table and leaning closer to Alex.

"Are you going to kiss me?" she asked, holding his gaze.

He visibly swallowed before nodding and closing the distance between them.

Susie closed her eyes, letting herself absorb the sensation of Alex's soft, full lips as his mouth began to explore hers. He shifted, placing his arm around her waist and pulling their bodies closer together. Their teeth clashed and she pulled back. She should be pulling his clothes off by now; instead, she was thinking about how awkward the whole thing was.

Squaring her shoulders, she leant in again, letting her hands slip into Alex's dark hair, tangling it around her fingers as she sought the pleasure that came with a decent kiss.

Rationally she understood that there was nothing wrong with Alex's technique. She just couldn't seem to find her rhythm, and when their teeth clashed again, she eased back, placing her forehead against his with a sigh.

"This isn't going to happen, is it?" Alex asked.

Susie shook her head. "I'm sorry," she said quietly.

"Don't be," he said, shaking his head earnestly. Moving, he adjusted his fly and she felt a surge of guilt for leading him on.

"I don't know what's wrong with me," she said quietly.

"There's nothing wrong with you," Alex said. "You're perfectly entitled to change your mind."

Susie gave him a half smile, wondering how she'd been lucky enough to meet such a decent man.

"Now, I really did mean what I said about enjoying your company, so why don't we watch a movie? I think I have some microwave popcorn somewhere."

"I won't change my mind again," Susie said, feeling the need to be really clear with Alex after what she'd just done.

"I know," he said. "It doesn't mean we can't be friends, though."

She studied him for a beat, trying to sense his level of sincerity, and eventually she nodded. "That would be great, thank you."

CHAPTER TWENTY-THREE

Twisting in his sheets, Dean wished he had some way of cooling off. The very few truly baking days in London every year made air conditioning a luxury he'd never been able to justify, but he should have been sensible enough to buy a fan. After he'd slopped around his flat gulping whisky, he'd flung the materials he'd bought Susie into his office. He'd been trying to think how to give her the gift of all the things she'd been eyeing covetously at the shop without her feeling like he felt sorry for her. He just hadn't been able to resist calling the store to arrange for them to be delivered to him at work when he'd realised just how tough things had been for her. Some stupid part of him had obviously thought he could make up for the accident by buying her some brushes and stuff. What an ass.

He hadn't bothered with his duvet when he'd climbed into bed a couple of hours earlier, but a sheen of moisture still covered his skin. Despite his best efforts, his state of drunkenness wasn't anywhere near the level he'd intended, so he'd flung himself on the mattress and willed himself to fall asleep. Unfortunately, it hadn't worked, so instead he tortured himself with thoughts of Susie with Alex. The guy was a good colleague, and on his way to becoming a friend, but he wasn't good enough for Susie. He snorted to himself. As if he had any idea what Susie needed anymore.

Shifting in an attempt to find a cool spot on his mattress, he froze at the sound of the door to his flat opening. The sound of Susie moving around made him sit up. He was halfway to his bedroom door before he stopped himself. What was he going to achieve by confronting her now? Yet again, he was stuck with completely conflicting feelings. One part of him wanted to go to her and plead for forgiveness for his appalling behaviour, and he knew it had been appalling, no matter what he tried to tell himself. The other part knew that he couldn't face her yet. He had no idea how to fix things between them, and he certainly wasn't ready to hear her insights into his own pathetic attempts at relationships.

He lifted his phone to check the time as he sank back into his bed. It was just after eleven. Far earlier than he'd thought she'd be back. A small smile crossed his lips. The date couldn't have gone that well.

"Urgh, what?" Dean muttered, flinging his arm over his eyes as light spilled across his face.

"Exactly," Susie said, her tone making it clear his morning was only going to get worse.

Dean prised his eye open, cursing that last night's whisky had been enough to make itself known this morning, despite denying him the oblivion of getting adequately drunk. Susie, her short hair dishevelled, and a paint-covered smock over her pyjamas, was waving around the packet of paintbrushes he'd put in her studio the night before. He suddenly wondered when he'd stopped thinking of it as his office.

"What. Are. These?" she asked, punctuating the question with her irritation.

He raised his eyebrows and met her gaze. "They. Are. Paintbrushes," he said, matching the cadence of her words, if not the tone. Closing his eyes again, he draped his arm back over them. "I would have hoped you'd be able to recognise paintbrushes by now."

"I know what they are," she said.

Dean opened his mouth to point out she'd been the one to ask, but she beat him to it.

"What I meant was, why are these in your office?" Susie asked, continuing before he could get a word in. "And not just these; there are paints and a whole bunch of other things that I certainly didn't buy."

"They're for you," he said, the words coming out on a sigh. He'd known the moment he'd arrived home days ago, with all the supplies Susie hadn't been able to afford, that he had no way of giving them to her without her feeling like it was some sort of charity, when that couldn't have been further from the truth.

"What?" she asked. It seemed she was defaulting to question mode this morning.

He tried to summon up the brain power to answer her in a way that wouldn't just annoy her more, but his thoughts were fuzzy and the remnants of the whisky had left his head pulsing in a way that made him want to curl up and ignore the world for a while. "They are my clearly misguided attempt at an apology," he said.

"What?"

She really needed to stop asking him questions, as he knew if he kept talking he was going to end up saying something he'd regret again. Without a fully functioning brain, it was inevitable.

"I know how much this stuff cost. That's not appropriate," she said.

"Look," he said, shifting in his bed, the movement making him feel a little nauseous. "I know you have this thing about wanting to pay your own way for everything and never taking something from someone else, but it wasn't that much for me."

Susie flinched, and he realised he'd done it, he'd made things worse. Her head came up, her chin jutting out. "I don't need you to buy me stuff," she said. "I need you to be sorry for the way you spoke to me last night."

Dean closed his eyes for a few seconds, hoping to find his balance. "I'm sorry," he said. "I'm sorry we aren't close enough anymore that you feel I can tell you when I think you could be happier. I'm sorry that I said things the way I did and hurt you." He forced himself to open his eyes and meet her gaze, hating the sadness that seemed to radiate from her but determined to be truthful. "But I'm not sorry for being honest with you," he said. "I think you're trying to be someone you're not, and I want you to be happy."

At that she laughed, a harsh sound. "You think *I'm* trying to be someone I'm not?" she said, holding his gaze. "I think you need to look closer to home first. And you can't buy your way to forgiveness."

She crossed the room, dumping the paintbrushes on his bed as she went, and slammed out of the door. Dean rubbed his eyes, before moving to the drawers on the other side of his room. Pulling open the top drawer, he began to root around for the half packet of paracetamol he was sure he had in there. Finding it, he sighed with relief before popping two tablets in his mouth and swallowing them dry.

The door to his room swung open, moving so fast it hit the wall with a bang, rebounding slightly as Susie barrelled back in. For a brief moment she froze, her gaze travelling the length of his body, and if it wasn't for the look of stunned appreciation in her eyes, he'd have felt self-conscious standing there in his fitted boxers. He had a sedentary job, so he worked hard at keeping fit. He hadn't ever considered that Susie would be witness to the results, but he couldn't deny a little satisfaction at the way her eyes briefly glazed over.

"You didn't buy these last night," she said, blinking as she pulled her thoughts back to what had her storming into his room again.

Dean frowned at the small piece of paper in her hand. They might be in London, but specialist art supply shops were pretty unlikely to be open in the evenings, even in the country's capital, so he wasn't really sure what her point was.

"This receipt is from last week," she said, waving the slip around.

He rubbed his palm over the top of his head. "Yes," he said slowly, feeling like whatever answer he gave he'd be stepping onto some kind of landmine.

Susie frowned at him. "Why did you buy this last week? And don't tell me it was as an apology; there wasn't anything to apologise for then."

He met her gaze at that; her words last night had made it clear he'd had something to apologise for last week, something enormous, and something that he should have apologised for years ago, but if she didn't want to discuss it, he was happy to ignore it a little longer too. "Your work is amazing," he said. "I wanted you to have everything you could possibly need so that everyone can see just what you're capable of."

He dropped his gaze to the floor, figuring that being honest was the only way he could answer that question, but it made him feel oddly vulnerable to admit that he'd just had this impulse to do something nice for her, something that could help her achieve everything he knew she could.

He glanced back up at the realisation she'd sunk onto his bed. The sight of her sitting there, her shoulders rounded as she picked up the packet of paintbrushes she'd discarded earlier and turned them in her hands, stirred some protective instinct in him. He wanted to bundle her into his arms and never let her go.

"I can't afford to pay you back for these," she said finally, the words so soft he'd had to strain to make them out.

"They're a gift," he said. "You're not supposed to pay people back for gifts."

"But ... no one ... I don't get," she began, seeming to start half a dozen sentences before her words stalled, as though she didn't know what to say. That was so out of character for the Susie he knew that he moved across the room and sat next to her on the bed, his hand curling around hers as she held the paintbrushes. She turned to face him, but he kept his attention on their joined hands.

"Please," he said, without looking at her. "Just let me do this one small thing for you."

"It's not small, and you're already letting me stay here rent-free," she said, finding her voice again and reassuring him in the process. "It's not like I'm even doing your cleaning for you," she added, when he opened his mouth to speak. "You tricked me into thinking it would be at least a little bit possible for me to help you out in return."

Dean grinned at that. "I never said you could do the cleaning; you just assumed. Besides, Dylan needs the money. You wouldn't deprive a poor student of his income, would you?"

Susie's lips quirked in a smile that she was clearly fighting.

"Seriously, though, even if that wasn't the case, exactly when would you have time to clean?" he asked. "You already work every hour available on top of doing your placement."

Susie leant back, her hands falling to her sides as she let her body rest on Dean's bed, her legs dangling over the side. He let himself join her. "When was the last time we did this?" she asked.

Dean almost flinched at the question, but her tone made it clear she wasn't trying to pass judgement, it was just an observation. "Too long," he said, shifting his arm until he took her hand in his, simply lying next to her and holding hands like they had done more times than he could remember, before he'd been too afraid to face her. "To be fair, we need some Bruce Springsteen or Florence and the Machine playing loudly if we want to really recreate our youth."

He felt more than saw the smile that stretched across her face and let the warmth of her hand squeezing his float through him, but he couldn't answer her smile with one of his own. One thought kept creeping to the front of his thoughts. What had the last few years been like for Susie that she didn't know how to accept a gift?

CHAPTER TWENTY-FOUR

Stirring at the sound of the front door opening, Susie realised she'd fallen asleep on the couch again.

Well, she figured that was what back-to-back shifts crammed around her time in Sam's studio would do. She hadn't managed more than five hours' sleep a night for the last week, and despite the fact she was used to working hard, she was grateful for the fact she didn't have to work the next day.

Sitting up, she found a smile for Dean, his tie loosened around his neck and his top button undone, making him look more casual, more real, than he'd looked for a while.

"You work too hard," he said, taking in the Mojo polo shirt and obviously concluding that she'd crashed after her shift at the pub again.

Blinking at her watch, Susie realised it was three a.m. "I could say the same to you," she commented. "Have you just finished work?" She frowned; she knew Dean wanted to sort his coding issue out, but surely he wasn't going to be any use to anyone after working for nineteen hours straight.

He didn't answer her comment. Instead, he just grinned at her. Tilting her head to one side, Susie realised that, despite the presence of the almost permanent shadows under his eyes, he looked happier than she'd seen him look in years.

"You did it?" she asked.

His smile grew broader.

"You fixed the code?"

He nodded and her own exhaustion fell away. Jumping to her feet, she crossed the room and threw her arms around him.

"I knew you'd do it. Congratulations."

His arms slipped around her waist and he spun her around. "Well, you had more faith in me than I did."

The words were whispered so close to her ear that the feel of his breath sent a shiver down her neck and heat through her body — a reaction to Dean she'd sworn was relegated to the past. Feeling suddenly awkward she pulled back, and plastering on a smile, looked towards the kitchen. "This calls for a drink to celebrate."

As though reading the shift in her mood, Dean took a step back and rubbed his hand over his cropped hair, his face darkening. "I'm sure you're tired; we can celebrate another time."

"Nope," Susie said, walking to the kitchen. "This is huge. We're celebrating now."

As though the shadows had receded, he smiled again and followed her.

Looking through the cupboards, Susie realised she hadn't seen anything resembling a liquor cupboard since she'd been staying at Dean's place.

"What are you looking for?" he asked, leaning against the breakfast bar as he watched her hunting through his things.

Pulling her eyes from the way his tall frame filled the suit trousers and shirt, she turned back to the cupboards. "This calls for something a bit more special than a beer," she said, her voice muffled by the corner unit she had her head stuck into. Pulling her head back out, she realised he was watching her.

"There's some champagne in the cupboard above the oven."

"Perfect," she said, studying the cupboard in question and trying to get her sleep-deprived brain to figure out how to reach high enough to get anything out of it.

"It'll be warm," Dean said, his voice suddenly right behind her.

Swallowing hard, Susie cleared her throat before replying. "I'm sure warm champagne will be nicer than the warm scrumpy we used to drink."

The warmth of his chuckle seemed to rumble through her as he leant over her to grab the bottle from overhead. "Or that schnapps Nathan and Maggie stole," he said. "One sip was enough for us; no idea how the pair of them finished the whole bottle."

Instead of answering, Susie took the opportunity to put some space between them by grabbing two glasses from the other side of the small kitchen and heading back to the lounge. "To your brilliance," she said once Dean had poured them a large glass each.

"I'll drink to that," he said with a laugh, clinking his glass to hers before taking a large swallow.

"I can't believe that you're so fancy now that you just have bottles of champagne sitting around in your cupboards," Susie said with a smile.

"If I was properly fancy, they'd be chilling in the fridge," he said.

"That would mean you expect to have people around, though," she said, "and from what I can tell, that's something that doesn't really happen."

"I have people round," he said, frowning at her.

"Go on then, when was the last time you had someone round?" Susie asked, interrupting as he opened his mouth to answer. "And I don't count."

Dean closed his mouth for a beat. "Firstly, you very definitely count, and secondly, Niall was here last week."

Susie rolled her eyes. "People you didn't invite don't count either. Go on, when did you last invite someone here?"

He frowned, his mouth opening and closing a couple of times, as though he'd come up with an answer before realising it wasn't the right one. "Honestly, I don't know if I've ever invited anyone here," he said.

"Okay, let's not get into debating whether or not we're living our best lives again," Susie said. "I'm enjoying being friends too much to let anything spoil it, especially when we have celebrating to do." Carrying the bottle and her glass to the lounge, Susie sank into the sofa. Grabbing a second bottle, Dean joined her.

"I'm enjoying being friends again too," he said, focusing on placing the bottle on the table as he said the words.

"Good," she said, "because you might have managed to get rid of me once, but you're not going to be able to pull that off again."

Dean looked up at her words. Her smile reached her eyes in a way that reassured him she meant it.

By the time they were nearing the bottom of the second bottle, Susie leant forward, her elbows on her knees and her chin in her hands as she stared him down. "So, fun as this is, you need to celebrate properly, so what's the plan?"

"Well," he said, "I have a bit of money saved, and with the bonus they've promised me for fixing this, I could afford a sports car."

"Ooh," she said. "I thought you didn't bother with a car in the city, but that sounds like a plan."

"I know, I suppose I've always thought it was a bit indulgent," he said, still uncertain what had made him say it.

"Given the supercar posters you always had covering your half of the bedroom you and Nathan shared growing up, I'm surprised you haven't bought one before," she said, turning her head to take in his flat, before turning back to him. "I'm sure you'd have been able to afford one before now."

Dean shrugged, not wanting to admit just how terrifying the thought of having a car, and having to drive it, made him feel. Somehow, with Susie here, her fearless enthusiasm for life made him believe anything was possible.

"Do you know what car you want?" she asked.

"Not really," he said. "There are a few that have been on the wish list since I had those posters, but I don't know what I'd go for." He'd never allowed himself to even consider it.

"Well then," she said, bouncing on the chair. "We need to book you some test drives so you can figure it out."

Dean leant back, his enthusiasm waning at the realisation he'd actually have to follow through. "I haven't driven for a really long time," he said, taking a sip from his almost empty glass to cover his sudden nervousness.

"I'm sure it'll be fine," Susie said, studying him in a way that made him wonder just how successful his efforts to remain relaxed and casual had actually been. "If I admit a secret to you, will you promise to try a test drive?"

He frowned; just how obvious had his nerves been, and did she realise what was causing them? The more he spoke about it, the less he was up for driving anything, but his curiosity won out. If Susie was willing to share a secret with him, he certainly wasn't strong enough to leave that alone. He nodded.

"You were right," she said. "My secret is that you were right."

He felt his frown deepen.

"What you said to me the other night," she said, waving her not empty enough glass around and letting a little of the champagne slosh over the side and onto the carpet. "I date men who are safe, reliable, and if I'm honest, a little bit boring."

"So, your date with Alex?"

"Was fine, the meal was good, what we had of it. I actually invited myself back to his place before we'd ordered our mains," she said, her cheeks going pink. "I thought sleeping with him so soon would be a good way to prove to myself that I still knew how to have fun, that I was still the person who'd do something I knew I shouldn't just for the hell of it."

Dean felt himself still; the idea that his words had caused her to do that made his stomach churn. He really shouldn't have had so much to drink if he was going to have to face the fact his words had made Susie do something that didn't reflect just how much she was worth. She was more than entitled to sleep with whoever she wanted, and he wasn't going to investigate why that thought made him want to puke. It was the idea of her doing it to make a point, rather than because it was what she truly wanted, he decided.

"The worst of it was, the moment we started kissing, I knew it wasn't going to work out," she said with another shrug.

"Did you…?" Dean asked, the words breaking as he spoke. He cleared his throat and tried again. "He didn't … you know?"

Susie smiled at that. "No, he was a perfect gentleman. We watched a movie," she said.

Dean felt something inside him uncurl. She hadn't slept with Alex, and Alex had respected her choice. He should have known the guy wouldn't do anything that wasn't consensual, but for a heart-stopping moment he'd wondered. "You won't be seeing him again, then," Dean said, once the relief that she hadn't slept with his friend sank in.

"Oh yes, I'm sure I will," she said with a smile. "We've decided to be friends."

The short-lived relief seemed to sweep away; of course Alex had agreed to being friends. He was obviously hoping for a chance to turn that into more. "So," Dean said, fixing Susie in his gaze, determined not to let his bizarre reaction to her love life spoil their evening. "I'm pretty sure you just admitted that I was right. I think you probably owe me a dare for that."

Her eyes widened. "We haven't done that for years," she said, her words slow, cautious.

"Chicken?"

"Am not," she said, squaring her shoulders. "What's the dare?"

"I'll need some time to come up with something just right."

"That's not fair, you can't expect me to agree to some unknown dare," she said.

Dean put his empty glass down and held her gaze. "You'll just have to trust me," he said.

Susie scowled at him, but the flush that covered her cheeks let him know she was on board with his suggestion, even before she nodded her agreement. "You have a week to come up with something, or you forfeit," she said.

"It's a deal," he said, holding his hand out to shake hers, cementing the agreement.

He was going to have to think hard to come up with something just right. He had a feeling whatever he picked was going to determine whether she embraced the fun side of life again or hid away from it for good this time.

CHAPTER TWENTY-FIVE

Putting her phone away, relieved at the regular 'everything's fine' message from her mum, Susie pulled her new packet of paintbrushes out of her bag, before delicately placing them in the corner of her workstation. Just seeing them there sent a wave of joy through her — both at the sentiment behind the gift and the brushes themselves.

"Wow," Laura squealed as she registered them. "When did you get Kolinsky brushes?"

"They are excellent tools," Charles said, waving one of his own set at them.

"Dean bought them for me," Susie said, feeling the heat in her cheeks at the admission. It was strange to find herself on the receiving end of such a generous gift, and any concern she'd initially had that they'd been some sort of bribe to get her to forgive his outburst, or worse, some kind of pity gift, had passed at his awkward admission about wanting to help her.

She met Laura's and Charles's gazes in turn, half daring them to suggest she shouldn't have accepted them.

"He's so dreamy," Laura said, her eyes glazing slightly and causing Charles to clear his throat. "Oh, don't worry," she said, her curls bouncing as she turned to face him. "He's too old for me."

Susie laughed at the look on Charles's face.

"And you're the only man I'm interested in," Laura added, slipping her hand into Charles's and giving Susie a shy smile.

Susie smiled warmly back; she was delighted for the young pair and hoped they made the most of their time together, before they had to head back to the reality of normal life.

"He's a good friend to you," Charles said, moving closer to inspect Susie's new brushes, without letting go of Laura's hand.

Susie nodded, but suddenly couldn't find her voice. At some point, she knew she and Dean were going to have to address their past. Their newly blossoming friendship would be shallow and fragile if they didn't deal with that. She just didn't want to have to admit to just how much he'd hurt her. It was bad enough that she'd blurted out a hint at it when he'd called her out for dating Alex the other night; that had been enough vulnerability for a lifetime.

"Fancy joining us for dinner after this session?" Laura asked, moving away to start work on her own piece.

Susie shook her head. "I'd love to, but I'm helping Dean with something before I start my shift at the pub later."

She only hoped Dean was going to stick to the plan to go and look at cars, instead of springing whatever dare he'd come up with on her. It'd seemed like such a simple thing to agree to at the time, but now her stomach swooped whenever her thoughts drifted to it. The things they'd done when they'd been younger had been just the right side of the law, and when they hadn't been, they'd been young enough to get away with their antics being dismissed as the hijinks of youth. They wouldn't have that excuse anymore. The only saving grace was that at least no one from home would know. She was still working hard to be seen as reliable and trustworthy. She couldn't risk anything unravelling her years of work.

Standing at the door of the showroom, Dean sucked in a breath; he knew he'd been the one to raise the subject the other night, but he was seriously regretting it now. The sight of the sleek vehicles did little to settle his nerves.

Despite the fact it was a total cliché, he wanted a sports car. It was one of those foolish childhood dreams that just wouldn't go away, although the very idea of sitting in the driver's seat made him break out in a cold sweat.

Susie, seemingly oblivious to his inner turmoil, pushed past him, grabbing his hand as she headed towards the nearest car.

"Okay, so do you have a particular car in mind, or is it just 'generic sports car' that you want?" She smiled at him, and he realised that she'd sensed his tension, but in her usual way was just barrelling through it. She'd never needed to understand why someone was struggling to help them with their challenges. Unfortunately, he knew this wasn't something he could get past. And now he was here, he felt foolish for even considering it. He didn't deserve to move on from this.

"Nothing specific," he said, rubbing his hand over his hair and forcing a smile. He should be delighted; he'd solved the biggest problem his company had faced for years and was in line for a serious bonus, as well as the points this would have earned him for when they decided who to give the new partnership to. Yet, standing in the doorway of the high-end dealership, he could feel sweat beginning to trickle between his shoulders. His legs felt like lead weights as he followed Susie.

She walked them around the whole showroom and despite himself, he found he began to enjoy looking at the sleek models. Peering into the windows, he took in the variety of cockpit designs. The seats looked like they belonged on a racetrack, but some of them had the kind of padding that made it obvious they were built for comfort, as well as speed.

"Would you like any assistance?" A groomed man walked up to them, his smile relaxed and genuine.

"Um, we're just looking around for now. Is that okay?" Dean answered.

"Of course, and feel free to sit in them and have a good poke around if anything catches your eye."

"Thanks," Susie said brightly.

"Can I get you a drink while you look?" the man asked.

"I'm good. Do you want anything, Dean?" Susie asked, turning to him.

Dean shook his head and the man walked away, leaving them to their browsing.

"I can see you in a car like this," Susie said, pointing to a sleek black Porsche that looked like a modern version of the one he'd had a poster of.

Dean swallowed and nodded.

Susie tilted her head to one side, studying him. He turned away and focused on the gleaming display of alloys that graced one wall. That was easier than looking at the cars, than letting the fear of what damage he could do if he climbed behind the wheel keep creeping up on him.

"Why don't you try the seat, see if it's as comfortable as it looks?" Susie's voice pulled his gaze back in time to see her swinging the low door open.

Dean stared at the driver's seat. He'd been in plenty of cars since the accident, but he didn't know if he would ever be able to get in the driver's seat again. He didn't deserve to. "Why don't you try it?" he asked, raising his eyebrows at Susie, infusing his voice with an amusement he didn't feel, before adding, "You'll look a damn sight sexier in it than I will."

She frowned at him, before smiling. "Okay, I'll do it if you do."

No, there was no way he could sit in that seat.

"Come on, you have to take a picture of me for my mum, and I know she'd love one of you," Susie said, smiling at him, one side of her lips curled up in the way he knew meant she was determined to get her own way. "It's not like we have to worry about damaging it; we aren't going to get far without the keys."

Swallowing hard, he nodded. "Me first," he said, knowing if he waited, he'd lose his nerve.

Susie was right, the car wasn't going anywhere, it was no different to sitting on his couch at home. He could do this. Taking a deep breath, he stepped forward and sank into the seat. He often imagined he could feel the sensation of the bucket seats on his old Vectra, but this was like a parallel universe where everything and nothing was the same. He was sitting in the driver's seat of a car again, and yet the way the chair cushioned him, curling around his sides in an embrace, made it feel as though he was in a massage chair, not a machine capable of taking someone's life. Closing his eyes, he fought the memories that pressed in on him but before he knew it, he'd leapt out of the vehicle and stalked out of the showroom.

Standing with his back to the wall, Dean rested his hands on his knees and focused on controlling his breathing. He didn't know how long he'd stood there, but he suddenly became aware of someone gently rubbing his back.

Susie stood at his side, her expression patient, gentle, but thankfully free of pity. "When was the last time you drove a car?" she asked, her voice quiet, but the intensity of the question ensuring it cut through the noise of the city.

"That night," he said, the words almost a whisper. He turned his gaze to the green space opposite them. He hadn't driven since the night he'd killed that poor woman. No, she had a name: he'd killed Louisa Smithson — he'd taken her life, he wasn't going to take her name from her as well.

"You know it wasn't your fault," Susie said.

"She's still dead," Dean said flatly.

"She was drunk, speeding, and emotional. We're lucky she didn't kill *us*," Susie said.

Dean didn't answer. He'd heard all the logic before: the police investigation, their findings that Louisa Smithson had been drinking heavily, and after a row with her husband had climbed into her car and driven erratically enough to take out a post-box and half a hedge before finally coming to a stop when her car had collided with Dean's. Rationally he understood that he couldn't have stopped the accident, but it didn't stop him from seeing that moment every time he considered driving again. Part of him longed to have that freedom back, to be able to just climb into a vehicle and go, but he didn't deserve it.

"If I'd reacted faster, she wouldn't have hit us at all," Dean said, his eyes falling to Susie's legs, to the memory of the damage that collision had inflicted on the girl who'd been unfortunate enough to be in the car with him, the damage that he was sure the woman standing in front of him still lived with.

"Do you feel guilty that I was in that car?" she asked.

He dropped his gaze to the floor at that, taking in the sight of ground-in gum and the build-up of dirt that seemed to mark every pavement in the city.

"Dean." His name was almost a plea on her lips, and he found himself looking up to meet her intense gaze. "I spent a long time feeling guilty that I made you go out that night," she said, her gaze holding his.

He shifted, straightening his stance so he was looking down at her again. Yes, it had been her idea to head into Bristol that night, but she'd been having a bad day, she'd been cleaning holiday cottages that summer. One of the guys in their year at school had been back from university for the summer, and had taken the opportunity to let Susie know he thought she didn't deserve to do anything more than clean up after what he'd termed her betters. She'd been so upset that Dean knew he'd have done anything to make her smile. She might have suggested they go out, but they did it all the time; it wasn't her fault he was on that road that night.

"But…" he began, not knowing how to articulate how ridiculous she was being to even consider that she held any share of the blame. "It wasn't your fault," he finally managed.

Susie gave him a small smile. "I know. It took me a long time to come to terms with that, and I have, mostly, but it wasn't your fault either," she said. "It was awful, and tragic, but it wasn't your fault."

"I was driving," he said.

"You deserve to move forward, to make the most of your life," Susie said, her free hand lifting to cup his face. "If you don't want to drive, that's no one's business but yours, but I think you do. I think you want a car, and you want to hop in and drive whenever the mood takes you, like you used to love doing, but this misplaced guilt is stopping you."

Dean shook his head in tiny movements to get his point across without losing the warmth of Susie's palm against his cheek.

"Dean, you are a funny, kind, warm, generous man, you deserve a good life."

He stared into her eyes, a burning in his chest that was so alien that for a split second he wondered if he was having a heart attack, but no, it was just Susie. It wasn't even her words, it was the fact she seemed to be able to see right into his soul, as though his every fear and secret, every dream was laid bare to her. For a heart-stopping moment, he wondered if he could get Susie to really and truly forgive him. Perhaps if he could, he'd be able to forgive himself.

Blinking hard, he swallowed; he needed to change the subject. He didn't do vulnerable; he didn't allow himself to feel like this.

"You missed one," he said, letting his lips curl up at her confused expression. "I think sexy should have been on that list." He waited for her to drop her hand and smack his arm, the way she always did when they were younger. Instead, she stroked her thumb over his cheek before giving him a soft smile.

"I'll give you that one," she said, finally letting her hand drop.

Dean opened his mouth to say something, anything, he wasn't really sure what; he just knew he needed to know what that meant. Did she agree, or was she humouring him?

"I have a shift at Mojo to get ready for, and I think you need a drink. Why don't you come keep me company this evening?" Susie said, breaking into his thoughts, her question taking away the opportunity to ask the one that had been forming in his mind.

CHAPTER TWENTY-SIX

"You're serious?" Susie said, knowing she probably looked like a startled fish, but finding herself unable to do anything about it.

"Yes," Sam said, an amused smile on his face.

"But, seriously, you're serious?"

"Yes, Susie, I'm seriously serious. I want you to show your work at my exhibition."

"But…" she began, unable to string her thoughts together to form anything resembling a full sentence.

"But?" Sam asked, amused.

"But…" Susie said again.

"But nothing, your work is incredible, Susie," Laura said, her curls bobbing.

Even Charles was nodding enthusiastically.

Susie felt the heat in her cheeks as her lips finally slipped into a smile. She'd felt sick coming in this morning, knowing that Sam was planning to share the outcome of the placement with each of them. Now she didn't know what to feel. "Thank you," she said, not quite able to meet Sam's eyes.

"It's my pleasure, Susie," he replied. "Now, if past years are anything to go by, we won't get any work done for the rest of today, so let's go and celebrate with champagne in my kitchen."

"Oooh, I've never had champagne," Laura said, turning and heading towards the main house without waiting for anyone else.

Charles's head swung between Laura and Sam, as though not sure whether he should follow Laura or do the polite thing and wait for Sam.

"Go on," Sam said with a nod towards the door. "You can open the bottle; we'll be there in a few minutes."

Susie sank onto the stool she'd been using almost every day for the last few weeks and buried her head in her hands.

"You're supposed to be pleased, not upset," Sam said, his tone gentle.

Waiting for the tears that were threatening to recede, Susie sucked in a lungful of air, trying to gather herself.

"I am happy," she said, once she was certain she had herself under control again.

"You might want to tell your face that," Sam said with a grin.

"I'm just overwhelmed," she said. "I know this has always been a possibility from the placement, but I truly never considered that my work would be selected."

"Your work is exceptional, Susie," Sam said. "You have incredible technique, but the last couple of pieces you have produced have been so alive and vivid, they seem to scream with emotion. I've run this programme for the last five years and I've never seen anyone's work progress the way yours has."

"Thank you," Susie said.

"I'd like to take the credit, but nothing I've taught you would bring out that sense of feeling in another artist's work; it's all you."

Susie stilled; she had a sinking feeling she knew exactly who was responsible for her work transforming into something more meaningful. Having her best friend back in her life, and being open with him, had cracked the wall she'd carefully built up, and she was terrified about what that would mean for her work, and her heart, when he reverted to ignoring her.

Susie glanced at her phone as it pinged. Smiling at Dorothy's note that everything was fine at home and asking how she was getting on, she sent a quick text back to say she was fine, before turning her attention back to Sam.

"Come on, let's go and celebrate with Laura and Charles," he said.

Taking Sam's outstretched hand, Susie followed him through to the kitchen, pausing in the doorway to the main house at the sight of Laura standing in front of Charles, who had his back to a tall cabinet. Laura's hand was on his chest and she was on her tiptoes. She gently placed her lips on a startled-looking Charles's. The young man recovered his shock quickly, his arms wrapping around Laura and pulling her closer as he began to kiss her back.

"Pub?" Susie asked, sharing an amused smile with Sam. She might not be getting her happy ending, but at least Laura and Charles were.

CHAPTER TWENTY-SEVEN

A quick call from Laura and Charles to find out where their missing mentor and fellow student were had led to the pair joining Susie and Sam in the pub. They'd appeared, a beaming Laura dragging a sheepish but delighted-looking Charles in behind her. The multiple bottles of fizz Sam had ordered for them meant Susie knew she'd be paying for her fun when she had to be up at five a.m. for the early shift at the coffee shop, but right now, she was buzzing too much to care.

Walking into the flat, she frowned at the sight of Dean fussing around in the kitchen.

Glancing at her watch in surprise, she realised it wasn't later than she'd thought, so why was Dean home already? As she took in the music gently covering the sounds of his movements, and the way the breakfast bar had been set, as though for a fancy dinner, her good mood crashed.

"Oh, sorry," she said. "I didn't realise you had company this evening."

"I don't," he said. "I was waiting for you."

Blinking hard, Susie smiled. "You cooked for me?"

"I did," Dean said. "You mentioned that today was the day Sam was deciding who would get the show, and I thought we could celebrate together."

"How did you know I'd get it?" she asked, trying to think through the fuzz of afternoon drinking.

"Because you're amazing," he said. "And I figured if you didn't, we could commiserate together."

Susie burst out laughing at the wry note in his voice. It was reassuring that Dean lived in the real world, even while he'd had faith in her.

"So?" he asked when she stopped laughing.

She smiled, feeling the size of her grin stretching her cheeks. "I got it," she said.

Dean moved across the kitchen and wrapped his arms around her waist, spinning her like he'd done when they were teenagers.

"I missed you," she said, the words slipping out before she could stop them.

He froze, letting her slide down his chest, until her feet touched the floor. Meeting her gaze, he stared, as though trying to figure out how to let her down gently.

"Don't say anything," Susie said, heat filling her cheeks as she moved away from him. "What have you made?" She poked at the large pan, knowing full well it was some kind of pasta, but needing to put some distance between herself and her stupid comment.

"I missed you too, Susie," Dean finally said, the words quiet, but heavy with meaning.

She turned to look at him, not knowing what to say next, but he beat her to it.

"It's pasta with tomato and bacon sauce and a bit of every vegetable I had in the fridge," he said. "Not very fancy, but it'll taste good."

"Thanks, I'm starving," she said, and realised it was true. They'd missed lunch in their bid to consume all the champagne Sam kept buying.

"So, what did your mum say about your news?" Dean asked.

"I haven't told her," Susie said, knowing how bad that sounded, but she didn't want to tell anyone else. She definitely didn't want to admit to the fact she'd been in touch with her mum since getting the news and still hadn't told her.

"What? Well, okay, but what about Maggie?"

"I haven't told her either," Susie said, trying to figure out how to articulate her feelings about it. "I haven't told anyone about wanting to be an artist; they won't know what this means to me."

"They'd want to come and see the show, you know they would," Dean said, studying her with a frown.

"I just don't want to tell anyone; it feels as though it's a precious bubble that will pop if people know. I know that sounds stupid, but I don't feel strong enough to cope if they say the wrong thing, or don't like my work," Susie said, studying her trainers.

"But you told me," Dean said, moving closer to her, his bare feet just a single step from her own feet.

Susie nodded without meeting his eyes.

"Thank you," he said, making her head shoot up, her gaze meeting his own intense one, his pale blue eyes studying her with a focus that made her shiver. Clearly reading the question in her expression, he gave her a soft smile. "You are trusting me with your secret, with your dreams," he said, taking the final step so his body was almost touching hers. Placing his hands on her cheeks, he slowly lowered his head, closing the final distance between them; then his lips met hers gently and the world seemed to fade away. Instead of deepening the kiss, he held them both in place, before pulling back and resting his forehead on hers.

Susie's heart galloped; she'd never experienced anything so intense, and logical thought seemed to vanish. All she could think about was the feel of Dean's lips on hers, and his words. She realised that she did trust him; despite everything that had happened, he was the only person she trusted enough to share her dreams with.

CHAPTER TWENTY-EIGHT

Dean knew he needed to calm down, but damn it, he'd worked too hard to be passed over like this, and not just once, but twice. Without even thinking about where he was going, he shoved the door open to the stairwell and began to make his way down the twelve flights of stairs. It would be quicker to take the lift, but he couldn't face the idea of having to make small talk with any of his colleagues. He wanted to run or punch something. Maybe he could punch someone? Niall would do.

By the time he reached the ground floor, he could convince himself his pounding heart was a result of the exertion, rather than the shock he'd received.

Rounding the corner and exiting the building, he dashed into Ground Up and found himself standing in front of the counter, frowning at the realisation Susie wasn't there.

"Are you after Susie?" the long-haired lad serving asked him. He knew Susie had introduced them, but in his fog of emotion he couldn't remember his name.

Dean didn't know why he'd come here; he couldn't just turn up and intrude on Susie's working day. He needed to leave; he just needed to figure out where he was going to go.

"She's out back on her break," the lad said, just as Dean started to turn away. "You can go back if you don't tell anyone I let you through."

Dean gave the lad a grateful smile before heading to the door he'd indicated; the 'Staff Only' sign and keypad access suggested that Dean really shouldn't be going through, but he didn't care, and when he was able to just push the door open, his relief at being able to see Susie pushed out the fleeting thought that he didn't like the idea of her working somewhere with such lax security.

"Dean," Susie said, the surprise in her voice giving way to a genuine smile as she registered his presence.

He didn't speak; he couldn't work out what to say, how to justify his random appearance at her place of work.

"What's wrong? Come and sit down," she said, rising from a plastic chair next to a chipped Formica table that was at complete odds with the plush furniture in the café area of the coffee shop. He'd left for work before she'd been up this morning, and something in the back of his mind was screaming that he shouldn't have come here so worked up. She deserved better from him after he'd kissed her last night than a temper tantrum the next time she saw him.

He shook his head. He couldn't sit, he needed to do something, anything. He needed to fix this, but in his heart he knew he couldn't.

"Dean, you're starting to worry me," she said. "What's wrong?"

"They're going to give the partnership to Niall," he said, the words shooting out like bullets.

"What? Why? When?" Susie asked. "But why would they give it to Niall? You're the one who solved that problem."

"They've just spent the last forty minutes grilling me about why I want the job. They made it very clear they think I don't care enough about the company to be right for the partnership and that while they think I'm a great coder, they don't seem to think I'm ready for partner yet."

"What? You've worked stupid hours the whole time I've been here; how could you possibly care more?"

Dean shrugged.

"What did Niall say?" Susie asked. "I bet he's gloating like mad."

"They haven't given it to him yet," he said. "They're going to call later and tell us their final decision, but I know it's not going to be me."

Susie moved towards him and wrapped her arms around his waist, pulling herself against his taut frame. "You deserve better than that," she said.

For a beat, he didn't move, but as she began to rub small circles on his back with one hand, he felt himself begin to unclench, her warmth and support taking away some of the sting of rejection. "They've cancelled my bonus too," he said.

"What?" Susie's head snapped up, her vivid green eyes sparkling with an unexpected fury as she met his gaze.

"They said no one is going to get a bonus for at least six months because the time it took to fix the problem meant they've lost too much revenue."

"What a load of rubbish," she said. "They wouldn't be getting any revenue at all if it wasn't for you."

"It's not really the money," he said.

"I know," she said, holding his gaze. "I know you don't really care about the money. It's about being recognised for what you've done, for everything you created and have contributed to the company."

Dean blinked and tilted his head upwards, avoiding the intensity in Susie's expression. She understood him in a way that no one else ever did. Even his family thought he was obsessed with money; they'd never been able to see it was about being appreciated and valued, and impressing them.

The sound of his phone ringing pulled his attention back to the present.

"You should check that," Susie said.

"It'll just be work; I probably wasn't supposed to just walk off like that. It's not very mature," he said with a sigh.

"Stuff them," she said. "If they can't let you have a moment after kicking you in the teeth like that, then they definitely don't deserve you."

Still, he found himself reluctantly unwinding one arm from Susie's back and slipping his hand in his pocket while using his other arm to hold her in place, where he needed her, right against his chest. The display flashed with the only other number that could have made him feel worse in that moment. "It's Mum," he said, on a sigh.

"Why don't you answer? I'm sure she'll make you feel better," Susie said.

Dean laughed, the sound much harsher than he'd intended.

"What?" Susie asked, her brow wrinkled.

"If there was ever a worse time for me to listen to her ramble on about how amazing my brothers and their families are compared to me, I can't think of it." He knew he sounded bitter, and he knew he shouldn't have let his resentment over Grace's obsession with reminding him how much better his brothers were than him slip out, but he was at breaking point.

As Susie studied him, he clenched his jaw, needing to hold something back, needing to get a hold of his emotions before she served up whatever platitude she thought was going to help with the years of hurt. When she didn't speak, and simply tightened her hold on him, resting her head on his chest, he let out a breath he hadn't realised he'd been holding. This, just this, was all he needed.

He didn't know how long he'd stood there before Susie spoke again. "So, did you figure out my dare yet?"

He leant back to study her, wondering at the change of subject.

"Well, you're already playing hooky today," she said, giving him a cheeky smile. "I should probably join you in doing something ill-advised as well."

A smile curled Dean's lips as he realised she was trying to distract him. "I did have something in mind," he said. Spotting the small barred window, his smile broadened at the realisation it was a glorious day. At least that would make crossing the city more pleasant. "What time do you finish?" he asked, trying to remember if she had the evening off but desperately hoping she did now the idea of spending time together had been planted.

"I'm supposed to be on until six, and then I have a shift at the pub later."

His shoulders slumped. Well, there went that plan.

"Give me a minute," she said.

Dean stood in the café break room, trying not to let the frustration that had made him rush here return in full force. He was a grown adult; he could cope on his own for the afternoon.

"Okay," Susie said, returning and punching a number into one of the lockers that were stacked at the side of the room, before grabbing her bag out and turning to face him. "Let's go."

"But you have hours left on your shift," he said.

"I thought I could play hooky with you," she said with a smile.

Dean frowned at her. He had wanted her to start taking chances again, to start really enjoying life, but he didn't want to be responsible for her getting in trouble; he knew how much she needed the job, and had quickly sussed out that it wasn't because she spent a lot. He had a feeling she was sending just about every penny she earned back home.

"Don't panic," Susie said, smacking his arm. "It's too hot for people to want coffee today, so it's been really quiet. Momin was happy for me to take off early."

Dean relaxed at that, pleased that she'd gone out of her way to spend time with him.

"So, where are we going?" she asked.

CHAPTER TWENTY-NINE

Stepping out of Tower Hill station, Susie flapped the bottom of her polo shirt.

"Sorry," Dean said, matching her movements with his now untucked shirt. "We could have walked, but I want us to have time to enjoy this before you have to get ready for your shift."

Susie smiled, enjoying the sight of Dean a little rumpled before her concerns about what he had planned returned to the forefront of her mind. Taking a deep breath, she let him steer the way across the concrete paving slabs outside the station and through the streets.

"So, where exactly are we going?" she asked, finally giving in to her curiosity.

"You'll see when we get there," he said, giving her a smile and slipping his hand into hers.

The contact took away the sting of him still refusing to tell her what she was being expected to do. What would he consider something they shouldn't do, but that would be fun? And what could possibly require them to travel halfway across the city to get to it?

Heading down a wide road with industrial-looking railings on their left, Dean turned into a small side street that led to what looked like the back of a group of ageing commercial buildings and blocks of modern flats. CCTV and tall gates made the place look uninviting.

"Ready?" he said, giving her a grin that threw her right back to being a teenager.

Susie nodded, not really sure she was ready, but trusting that he wouldn't lead her too far astray.

Letting go of her hand, Dean headed straight for the gates that were clearly there to allow vehicle access. Sliding the locking mechanism and easing the gate open, Dean turned to her again. "Ta-da!"

"I don't think we're supposed to be here," Susie said, nervously looking around.

"Well, they should have locked it, then," Dean said with a shrug and another grin. Pulling her after him, he pushed the gate shut behind them and quickly crossed the concrete ground, leading them to what was obviously a fire exit for whatever was behind the blank wall it was placed in. Slipping his fingers along the metal edge of the door, he smiled again as it swung towards them.

"I *really* don't think we're supposed to be here," Susie said.

"Are you backing out?" Dean asked, raising his eyebrows.

Rolling her eyes, Susie shook her head. "No."

Dean stuck his head in the door, seemingly to check the place out, before he gestured for her to go through first. She wasn't completely sure that sneaking into somewhere was a good idea, especially when she had no idea where they were, but she wasn't about to let Dean think she'd lost her nerve.

The coolness of the building hit her as soon as she stepped over the threshold, but she barely registered it at the realisation that she'd just walked into a truly extraordinary theatre.

The arched room running the length of the space gave the interior the feel of being inside a giant barrel. Intricate mouldings and ironwork spread throughout the place in a way that hinted at functionality as well as decoration. The paintwork suggested a well-used, hard-working and historic venue that was nevertheless well cared-for. Pillars supported gallery seating areas on three sides of the room. The stage was topped by an arch that added to the sensation of being inside a barrel.

"Wow." Susie breathed the word, almost afraid to make a sound in the still place.

The seats were set out neatly throughout the main audience area, and Susie found herself wanting to see it in full flow.

"Thank you," she said, her hand slipping into Dean's.

"I'm glad you like it," he said.

"Where are we?"

"Wilton's Music Hall; it's an original Victorian music hall, but it was built inside a row of houses that were from the seventeenth century."

"It's incredible," Susie said, her head turning as she tried to take in the amount of history crammed into one place.

"Let's go check out the stage," Dean suggested.

Having assured herself that they were alone in the place, Susie headed towards the stage, taking in the layers of paintwork that should have been flaking from the walls, but somehow looked deliberate and completely finished. She longed to reach out and touch it but didn't want to risk damaging something so beautiful.

Walking up the small stairs to the first level of the stage, she realised that the stairs themselves moved, obviously to allow for different configurations depending on what show was being performed. The stairs to the main stage level seemed more permanent.

Turning around, she took in the view of the venue as the performers would see it. She could almost imagine the sea of faces, barely discernible against the brightness of the stage lights. She wouldn't want to do it herself, but she could understand how the roar of applause rolling off the curved walls in a place like this could fill the performers with the kind of high that made them want to keep performing.

At the sound of the instantly recognisable 'Dancing in the Dark' beginning to play, Susie turned to find Dean had connected his phone to the sound system for the theatre.

"Shh," Susie hissed, rushing across to turn the sound off.

"It's fine," Dean said, catching her as she neared him.

"What part of sneaking in involves making this much noise?" she said.

"Stop worrying," he said. "No one will be here at this time of day, and they have great soundproofing to keep the neighbours happy."

"Someone could be here," she said, shifting her head to look at the doors at the far end of the hall that were clearly the main entrance to the theatre itself. Beyond those doors there were bound to be offices and ticket booths and a bar.

"Better be ready to run if anyone appears, then," Dean said, giving her a grin.

"Dean, this is too much," Susie said. "Having a look around when the place was unlocked is one thing. Using their clearly expensive equipment while we're here is crossing a whole different line."

"Relax," he said. "What's the worst that can happen?"

"Oh, I don't know," she said, shrugging his hands from her arms and taking a step back. "How about we get arrested, end up losing our jobs and everyone decides I'm as much of a screw-up as my dad?" Susie froze; the last part of that statement had slipped out without registering with her brain, and the look on Dean's face made it clear he heard more than the words she'd spoken.

He took a step towards her, closing the small distance she'd created, gently pushing back the hair that had fallen into her eye. "Susie, I know I haven't done a great job of keeping you safe in the past. But I would never put you at risk of any of those things happening."

She opened her mouth, but the intensity of his statement made it impossible for her to reply.

"If it makes you feel better, I know one of the duty managers here. He unlocked the gate and door for us." Dean met her gaze with a wry smile. "I thought it would be more fun if you thought we'd snuck in. Sorry."

Susie frowned at him for a moment. "So, you're saying we have permission to be here?"

"Yes. I can show you the text messages proving it if it helps?"

She shook her head and smacked his arm. "You idiot," she said, equal parts frustrated that he'd let her worry and pleased that he'd gone to so much effort to create a *dare* for her. "But thank you." She realised that Bruce Springsteen had given way to her favourite song from the *Trolls* movie. "'Get Back Up Again'?" she asked. "Do you have my playlist on your phone?"

Dean laughed and pulled her into his arms. "No, but you've listened to the same songs enough since you've been staying with me that it was easy enough to put a few together for this."

Susie laughed in return as he spun her out and under his arm.

"Now, the real reason we're here," he said, giving her a sly smile. "You have a stage, you might not have the audience, but that doesn't mean you get away with not singing while you're up here. I dare you to put on a performance worthy of a sell-out crowd."

He studied her, clearly expecting her to refuse, and normally she would. The thought of singing in front of someone else would usually be enough to make her find any awful chore she'd been putting off. Dean was a different matter, though. He already knew she couldn't really sing, and she was sure he'd heard her singing along in the flat enough to know that she hadn't improved over the last few years. Besides, she'd already shared her most secret dream with him; singing would be a breeze after that.

"'Well, you can go ahead and bring it on'," she sang, belting the lyrics out in her off-key tone, her eyes fixed on Dean's until she turned and faced the rows of seats. Marching along to the beat, she paced from one side of the stage to the other, giving her movements as much flourish as she could manage.

Dean's clapping echoed around the space as soon as the song finished, and she gave him an unembarrassed bow.

"What else have you got on there?" she asked, gesturing to his phone.

They continued to work their way through the songs that Susie most enjoyed singing along with, and she was delighted when Dean joined her. Despite the fact his perfect pitch made her sound even worse, the sight of him leaping around the stage with her, his jacket and tie abandoned on the floor as they enjoyed the pretend admiration of the non-existent crowd, made her glad she'd gone for it when he'd thrown down the challenge. Seeing him have a good time, despite the disappointments of the day, was worth any embarrassment she might have felt at giving full volume to her attempts at singing.

The first notes of Lifehouse's 'From Where You Are' began to play, making Susie freeze. She loved this song, but she'd played it endlessly when Dean had walked away from her. The lyrics written to honour teenagers who lost their lives in vehicle accidents articulated the loss she'd felt when Dean had left after the accident. The lament to loss and pain was instantly out of place here, amongst their laughter.

Noticing that she'd stopped before reaching his phone, Dean moved over to her and put his hand on her shoulder. "Are you okay?"

Susie didn't want to have to explain what this song meant to her, how it would forever be associated with how much she'd missed him. She didn't want to spoil their afternoon by dredging up a past that neither of them could change. "Yes," she said, forcing a smile as she touched the screen, bringing it to life so she could skip the track. "I just thought we could do with something a bit more upbeat."

He gave her a look that made it clear he wasn't convinced. "You listen to this song all the time. I thought you liked it."

"I do," she said, touching the hand he'd placed on her shoulder reassuringly, before shifting out of his reach and giving him a wink. "But I definitely need to see more of your dancing."

"Stop," Dean said, reaching for her again. This time he placed his hands on her waist, holding her in place, despite the gentleness of his touch.

Susie studied the buttons on his shirt, not wanting to look at him, knowing that if she did she was going to have to face the conversation he was pushing for.

"We've ignored this for long enough," he said. "I need to apologise."

"No, it's fine," she mumbled.

"No, it's not," he said firmly, lifting one hand from her waist to her chin, lifting it until she was forced to meet his gaze. "I let you down, and I don't know if I can ever make up for that," he said. "But we need to talk about it."

Susie took a step back. She couldn't do this. She couldn't be honest about how she really felt, not if they had any chance of holding on to the tentative friendship they had created.

"Susie," Dean said, his tone gentle but determined. "I have loved having you in my life again, but I know if we have any chance of this working out, we have to talk about the past."

She shook her head.

"If you don't want us to be friends again, I'd understand."

Her head shot up at that. "No, that's not it. I do, I do want us to be friends again," she said. "I just don't know how to get through this conversation."

"That's easy," he said. "You let me do all the apologising, and hopefully, at the end of it, you agree to try to forgive me."

Susie blinked against the prickling in her eyes.

"I'm sorry," Dean said, moving to stand in front of her and sinking to his knees, his voice breaking on his words. "I'm sorry for the accident, and I'm ever sorrier for the fact you were hurt. I will never forgive myself for putting you in hospital."

She sank next to him and buried her face in her hands. "You really don't get it, do you?" she asked, meeting his gaze when she'd finally pulled herself together enough to speak.

He blinked at her, confusion crossing his face.

"The accident wasn't your fault; the fact I got hurt wasn't your fault. If anything, it was the opposite. The police were very clear that your fast reaction was the only reason I didn't die that night."

His eyes moved across her face, as though searching for the solution to something that didn't make sense to him. "But…" he said.

Susie held up her hand. "I don't want you to apologise for the accident; you don't need to. The fact you left me afterwards, that's what caused the most damage." She turned her attention to the rows of chairs spread out before them, unable to look at him. "You were my best friend and you just vanished, no goodbye — you didn't even come to see me in the hospital." The prickling in her eyes intensified and she blinked at the moisture that was there. She hadn't wanted to have this conversation, but now she'd started she couldn't seem to stop the words from coming. "You were the only person who was there for me, who understood me; you'd stood by my side through everything, and then you were gone."

"I did," Dean said, the words whispered.

She turned to find him watching his finger as he traced the grain in the floorboards.

"I came to see you in the hospital," he said. "That night, after the police had taken my statement, I went straight to see you."

Susie shifted to face him more fully. "I didn't know that."

Dean gave a weak smile. "It was about three in the morning. The police hadn't given me any information about how you were doing, and I was terrified for you. When I found you, you were knocked out with all the drugs they'd had to give you. You were wearing a faded blue hospital gown that was so big it was half hanging off your shoulder, and your leg was in a full cast, suspended from the bed. I sat next to the bed, willing you to be okay."

"I didn't see you."

"I held your hand," he said, swallowing visibly. "You were murmuring my name, so I kept saying that I was there, that it was all going to be okay. That was when you said you knew I'd keep you safe."

"I don't remember that," she said.

"I do. Those words were like being stabbed," he said, his throat bobbing as he swallowed. "There I was, the very reason you were in that hospital bed, and somewhere deep inside you had enough faith in me to believe I'd keep you safe."

Susie didn't speak, his words seeming to disconnect in her mind. Why would her faith in Dean make him push her away? Oh God, had she blurted something about how she really felt about him? Had some drug-induced admission of love sent him running? Back then, she'd been convinced that love didn't last and all romances were doomed to fail, which meant she'd never have acted on it, but he wouldn't have known that.

"Your mum came before I could figure out what to say," he said. "Seeing the depth of her worry made me realise that as soon as you woke up, you wouldn't feel that way about me anymore. When you woke up, you'd realise I couldn't be trusted to keep you safe, and I couldn't face seeing that. I couldn't face losing your respect and trust, so I left."

Susie frowned. Her mum had never mentioned Dean being at the hospital that night, not then and not in the months of grieving his departure that had followed. "That's not how I felt," she said, trying to make sense of it. "That was never how I felt."

Dean laughed, but the sound was harsh, making her flinch. "It was how you should have felt," he said. "I'd done the one thing I'd sworn I'd never do."

She gave him a questioning look.

"I know you only started hanging out with me so much after your dad left because you thought I could help you forget. I was the one kid you knew who'd help you rebel."

Susie opened her mouth, but Dean continued before she could interrupt.

"I didn't mind," he said with a shrug. "You were fun, and I liked that I could help you deal with everything just by being myself."

"I wasn't using you," she whispered.

"I know," he said, punctuating his words with a nod. "But you can't imagine what it was like to have someone like you seek me out, because you wanted me to be exactly who I was. You didn't try to change me. You weren't busy giving me *suggestions* about how I could be somehow better. Other than my granny, you were the only person who wasn't trying to change me back then."

Susie turned to study his profile. She'd known the adults around them had spent a lot of those years telling him to stop messing around, to grow up, be more mature and work harder, but she hadn't realised he'd carried that with him for so long.

"It didn't take long for me to accept that you might have sought me out for my reputation, but that you'd stuck around for me. I swore I'd never let anyone hurt you the way your dad did." Dean gave a bitter bark of laughter again. "And then I hurt you."

She reached out, letting her hand curl around his, but unable to find the right words for his confession.

"I was so sure you'd open your eyes and send me away, that you'd hate me for what I'd done to you, that I left."

Susie wiped her eyes, unable to shake the memory of him abandoning her, of all the times he'd avoided her in the years since. All the hurt she'd felt swelled up, and she pulled her hand back from his.

"I've spent years avoiding you, not wanting to give you the chance to tell me how much you hated me, not wanting to hear you say how much I'd hurt you. It got to the stage where I couldn't look at you without seeing the accident. I was too stupid to realise I was hurting you just as much by being so selfish."

"Losing you made the pain from the accident almost non-existent," Susie said, keeping her eyes on his profile.

Dean's head swung around, his pale blue eyes seeming brighter than ever in contrast to the red rimming them, liquid welling up and making them glitter. He studied her face, watching, as though trying to determine the truth in her words.

"Don't leave me again," she said, holding his gaze.

"I won't. I swear to you I won't," he said, leaning closer until his forehead met hers. "I promise I will never hurt you again," he whispered, wrapping his arms around her.

As Susie sank into his embrace, exhaustion seemed to wash over her, but it was a satisfied kind of weariness, one that spoke of finally shedding a weight she'd been unaware of carrying. "Don't do that," she said.

"Don't do what?" Dean asked, his tone anxious, the hand circling her back stilling.

"Don't make promises like that," she said. "Let's just agree we'll both do our best, and that you won't make assumptions about how I feel."

"I can agree to that," he said, and she felt his lips curl into a smile against her hair.

They were lying back on the well-worn floorboards, content not to speak, instead letting the music from Dean's phone wash over them when the lights sparked to life.

They jerked upright, giving each other a startled look. Leaping to her feet, Susie grabbed Dean's phone, causing the room to fall into abrupt silence.

"Let's go, before we get caught," she said, smiling as she held her hand out to him.

"You do remember that we're allowed to be here?" he asked.

Susie rolled her eyes at him. "But you were right, it's more fun to pretend we aren't."

"Says the woman who nearly had a meltdown at the thought of me using the speakers without permission," Dean said, but his tone was amused, and he let her drag him down the stage stairs and out of the fire exit they'd used to get in.

CHAPTER THIRTY

Watching Dean hang up the call, Susie didn't need to ask him what the outcome had been. His shoulders had slumped enough to make that obvious.

"I'm sorry," she said.

"They haven't made a decision yet," he said, meeting her gaze with a confused look.

"What? Why not?"

"I don't know, something about wanting to give us both more of an opportunity to prove ourselves now the coding issue isn't hanging over us."

"Well, that's good isn't it? It means you're still in the running."

"They aren't going to give it to me," he said, resting his elbows on the bar. "I'd have preferred them to get it over with."

"If they didn't have any intention of giving it to you, wouldn't they have just told you that?" Susie asked, wiping the bar top.

Giving Dean a quick nod, she headed further down the bar to serve the two women who'd just come in. They were so engrossed in their discussion that they barely looked at Susie as she passed their drinks over and processed their payment. Heading back towards Dean, she registered how exhausted he looked. While she felt lighter after their afternoon together, he seemed to be struggling even more. His phone call seemed to have brought all of his weariness back.

"Why do you want the partnership?" she asked, the question spilling out the moment it formed in her brain.

Dean looked up at her and blinked, as though surprised by the question, but surely he'd spent the morning discussing this with the existing partners — it couldn't be that hard to bring the answer to the front of his mind. "I've worked there for years. I'd like to be part of making it even stronger and developing its direction for the future," he said flatly when he finally answered her.

"Okay," Susie said, giving him a smile. "Thanks for the robot response. Now the real reason."

Dean studied the beer mat he'd been carefully peeling apart into layers. "Honestly," he said, "I don't really know. I've been coding for ages; going for partner is the next obvious step." His phone rang, and she could see him debating whether to answer it or let her keep quizzing him. "Hi, Mum," he said, speaking into his phone and giving Susie a half smile.

Well, that answered her unspoken question about how uncomfortable the conversation was making him. Despite the fact that he obviously loved Grace, he clearly had issues when it came to speaking to his mum.

Smiling, Susie dealt with another customer as Dean spoke in monosyllables into the phone. When he finally hung up, his shoulders had dropped even further. Deciding that, while he might not enjoy it, it would be good for him to work out why he really wanted the partnership, she returned them straight back to their conversation.

"Okay," she said. "What was the last thing that really got you excited at work?"

Dean sank into thought and Susie went to serve another group of customers. When she eventually made it back to Dean, she raised her eyebrows in question. He needed to be able to articulate this to himself if he was to have any chance of convincing the senior partners at work to give him a shot.

"Honestly, I had an idea for a programme that would add links to social media connecting people to the right support networks when they were viewing or posting about serious issues."

"How would that work?" Susie asked.

"Well, if you were looking at things about depression, it would add links for mental wellbeing charities."

"That sounds amazing. So, if you were looking at things to do with eating disorders, it'd have support groups for that?"

"Yes, and it'd be restricted to links for non-profit groups or companies so that it would be support that was genuinely available, regardless of your personal circumstances."

"How's it going, then?"

Dean frowned at her. "What do you mean?"

"I imagine there would be lots of development work needed and that sort of change would take time, so how is it going?"

"It isn't," he said flatly. "I pitched it to Elizabeth and Nigel, the senior partners at Social Software, and they said they weren't interested. There's no obvious way to make money out of it, so they don't want to put the resources into it."

"If you were a partner, could you make it happen?" Susie asked.

Dean frowned again. "I don't think so," he said. "The partners have to vote on projects, and they've already said no to it. I don't suppose my vote would change that. I did think about leaving and setting up on my own to create it." He blinked hard, as though surprised at his own words.

"Why don't you?" Susie asked.

"The same reason Social Software won't green-light it," Dean said, giving her a weak smile. "I don't know how to make money out of it."

"There's more to life than money," she said, knowing full well that it was easy to say that to someone who had plenty of it. When you didn't have enough, it could become an all-consuming focus.

CHAPTER THIRTY-ONE

"You really don't need to help with this," Susie said, for what Dean was sure was the millionth time.

"I really do," he said, giving her a half smile.

"You really don't."

"Why do you keep saying that? Don't you want me there?" he asked, knowing that wasn't the case, but enjoying the opportunity to wind her up.

"Well, you know," she said, waving her hands around. "This is going to be all about my work and things going well — if people like my art — and you're having a tough time."

"Susie," Dean said, stepping nearer and closing his hands around her upper arms, enjoying the sensation of being close to her. "I've had a rubbish time, but what sort of friend would I be if that in any way affected how much I support you?"

Her gaze fell as he stared into her eyes.

"Susie, I'm delighted for you, and I'll be even more delighted when you finally let me see what you've worked on for your final piece."

She'd been shut away in her studio at his flat almost every moment she hadn't been working since their afternoon at Wilton's Music Hall. Dean found himself intrigued by the way she'd almost completely lost herself in her work. He suspected that she wouldn't have even eaten if he hadn't forced her out whenever he'd been at home as well.

"Oh God, I hope you like it," Susie said, taking a step back, her face paling.

There was something about the vulnerability in her response that warmed him; she was finally letting him see her, rather than the cautious version of herself she showed the rest of the world.

"Assuming it's not a picture of one of my parents naked, or worse, both of them, I'm sure I'll love it. Your work is incredible," Dean said, slinging an arm around her shoulders as he steered her towards her studio. "Now, what needs doing?"

"Okay," she said, finally looking back up at him with a smile. "We need to get all of these canvases into my car."

Dean looked at the pile she gestured to, amused by the fact she couldn't even keep her precious artwork tidy.

"I'll take that one, though," she said, pointing to the large piece that was still on the table but hidden by the paint-stained linen cloth that covered it. "I don't know if Sam will want to show it, but it's coming anyway."

Dean grinned at the set of her shoulders, knowing that was the piece she'd spent the last week working on, and knowing that her determined statement was covering for her fear Sam wouldn't like it. Susie had sent him photos of it, and from the photos alone he'd insisted that she bring it so he could take a proper look and decide whether or not to include it in tomorrow's show, but evidently that wasn't enough to calm Susie's nerves about whether it was up to standard.

Helping Susie carry them down the hall, Dean paused at the door. "Have you shut Liquorice somewhere?" he asked, knowing the kitten would try to dart out the moment the front door swung open.

"No, I totally forgot," Susie said, meeting his gaze with a worried look.

"You track her down and I'll find the treats," Dean said, placing the artwork gently against the door before heading to the kitchen.

"I have her," Susie called. "I'll take her to my room."

Dean followed the sound of Susie's voice and pulled some of the miniature fish-shaped treats from the packet. Joining Susie in her bedroom, he grinned at the sight of her kneeling on the floor, cradling Liquorice. He popped the treats on the floor next to them, his smile growing as the kitten wriggled frantically to get out of Susie's hold. He wouldn't ever have thought of getting a pet, but he was secretly hoping no one claimed Liquorice. Once she was free, she pounced on the snacks, attacking them with the kind of effort that made it clear she was worried they would fight back if she didn't subdue them quickly enough.

With Susie giggling at Dean's side, they slipped out of her room, pulling the door firmly closed behind them.

Reaching Susie's car, Dean frowned. It wasn't tiny, but he wasn't sure they were going to fit the finished work in it.

"It'll be fine," she said, smiling at his expression. "I've transported things this size in it before."

He helped her fold the rear seats flat and remove the parcel shelf before letting her slide the work in. He was nervous that he'd judge the movement wrong and damage Susie's precious work.

"Should we bring some cushions to go under there?" he asked, studying the angle of the pictures and the triangle of space underneath them.

"I'm sure they'll be fine."

Dean frowned. "I think I'll get some anyway. We'd better not risk anything happening to your creations."

Susie stepped closer to him and slipped her arms around his waist as she stood at his side, studying the back of her car. "You're very sweet," she said.

He glanced down at the top of her head. *Sweet?* He'd been called a lot of things in his time, but sweet wasn't one of them. He let the word roll around his thoughts for a while, enjoying the sensation of Susie's arms around him, before deciding he liked being sweet for her. "I'll get the cushions while you get your last picture," he said, reluctantly stepping back from her embrace.

Slipping into the passenger seat, Dean was grateful that Susie hadn't raised the topic of him driving again since they'd been to the car dealership. He was content to sit back and let her be his chauffeur, and he didn't want thoughts of having to drive himself to spoil the time they had together.

"At least making the delivery this late at night means the traffic is lighter," Dean said, taking in the tension in Susie's posture as she navigated London's complex road systems.

"That definitely helps," she said, a quick grin crossing her lips.

"What do you fancy listening to?" he asked, fiddling with the dial on the dated radio that sat in the centre of Susie's dashboard.

Just as she opened her mouth to reply, his phone rang. A quick glance told him it was his mum and he muted the call, slipping the phone back into his pocket.

"You not going to answer that?"

"No, it's only Mum. I'll call her back tomorrow," Dean said, not wanting the inevitable gloom that followed a call with his mum to spoil Susie's evening. The show wasn't until tomorrow, but this would be the first time she'd be working with someone to get her work hung in a professional show, and he wanted every second of it to be wonderful for her. It had nothing to do with not wanting to have to explain that there was still no decision about the partnership to his mum. Nothing at all.

Even late at night, the journey to the gallery was quicker that Dean had expected, despite it being on the other side of the city to his flat. Once he'd helped Susie and Sam unload her work, he found a deep window ledge in the gallery space to sit and wait. He could answer a few emails while they took their time setting up.

"Sam said he's going to include my new piece tomorrow as well," Susie said, skipping over to him a short while later.

"That's brilliant," Dean said, standing to give her a hug. "Does that mean I get to see it now?"

"Um, well, I was hoping you'd wait until tomorrow," she said, blushing a deep red that made him wonder just what made her so reluctant to let him see it.

"I can wait twenty-four hours," he said, giving her a wink.

"It means we'll be a bit longer this evening. Sam and Edwina will need my help to rejig some of the displays so there is room for it."

Dean smiled over at Edwina, the woman who owned the gallery, and Sam, their dark heads bent closely together as they studied something on the table in front of them. "Take your time. I'm good here," Dean said to Susie. She thanked him and skipped back to the other pair.

Sitting back down, Dean leant against the cool glass of the window and stretched his legs out. When he'd finished all his emails, he figured he might as well listen to the voicemail from his mum.

As her gentle tone greeted him, his stomach swooped at her words. Without realising, he jumped to his feet. He had to go. He knew he had to go, and he had to go now, but he couldn't get his brain to work through how he was going to achieve that.

"Dean." Susie was holding his arms, but it took a moment for her voice to permeate his racing thoughts. "Dean," she repeated. "What's wrong?"

"Granny Agnes," he said. "She's in hospital."

"Oh God," Susie said, her face paling. "What happened? Is she going to be okay?"

"I don't know," Dean said, dragging his hands over his head. "She had a fall and she's had to go in." He sucked in a deep breath. "She's been asking for me," he said, his voice breaking with the guilt of not being there for his granny when she needed him.

"Okay, we need to get you there," Susie said.

He nodded, trying to gather his thoughts enough to work out the fastest way to get home.

"Do you need to get anything from the flat before we go?"

He frowned at Susie, trying to make sense of her words. "We?"

"Yes, we. I'm coming with you."

"You don't need to come; you have all this going on," he said, gesturing around the gallery. "I'll just get the train."

Susie stared at him, her eyebrows raised. "Even if it wasn't too late for any trains to be running back to the wilds of Honeyford, do you really think I'd let you deal with this alone?"

Dean studied her, knowing he should encourage her to stay, to make the most of every experience this opportunity was going to give her, but he couldn't make himself say it. Some part of him didn't want to face this without her at his side. The thought of losing his granny was one he couldn't even consider without wanting to break down completely, and it looked like Susie taking him in the car was the only way he'd be able to get there tonight. For the first time in years, he genuinely wished he still drove.

"I'm driving you, and we're leaving now," she said, looking to Sam, as if seeking his approval. At the other man's nod, Dean felt something in his heart loosen.

"I don't need anything from the flat. Mum keeps a few of all of our clothes at home just in case."

"Perfect, we can go straight from here," Susie said, slipping her hand into his as she led him out of the building.

CHAPTER THIRTY-TWO

The lights that lined the side of the motorway were far behind them, and Susie found herself stifling a yawn. It was a three-hour drive from London to Honeyford and despite the fact they were over halfway, Dean still hadn't said a word.

Glancing at the display on her dashboard for the hundredth time, she resigned herself to the fact they weren't going to make it to the hospital if she didn't stop for diesel. That was an expense she could do without. She'd been able to save loads by walking whenever her schedule had allowed her the luxury of saving the cost of a Tube journey, but as always, what she'd saved was stretched too thinly.

As they approached the services, she glanced at Dean, who continued to stare out of the window into the darkness. She let him know she was pulling in and would be as quick as possible, but he was so lost in his thoughts he barely looked in her direction.

Finally pulling up outside the hospital at three a.m., Susie easily found a parking spot and took charge, leading the way to the main reception desk.

Following the receptionist's directions down the labyrinth of corridors, they finally found themselves outside of the ward Agnes Parker had been admitted to.

As Susie raised her arm to ring the bell that would alert the nurses' station that there were people waiting to enter, Dean stopped her. She tilted her head up to look at him.

"What if…" he began, the words seeming to choke him. "What if she's…"

"Don't torture yourself," Susie said gently, raising her hand to his cheek. "Someone would have called you again if she'd died."

"But if she has and I wasn't with her…" he said, whispering the words as he held her gaze.

"Then she'd have passed away knowing that you loved her deeply anyway," Susie said, lowering her hand and resisting the urge to wrap her arms around him. The only thing that was going to help right now was finding out exactly how Agnes was doing. She silently prayed that the older woman was indeed still with them, but as Agnes was in her late eighties, it wasn't a sure thing. "Let's go and find out what's happened," she said, pressing the bell before Dean could stop her again.

His face paled at her action, but he squared his shoulders and nodded.

A young man in a grey striped tunic and trousers pushed the door open. "It's not visiting hours," he said quietly, frowning at them.

"I'm sorry," Susie said. "Agnes Parker was admitted earlier tonight, and we've driven straight from London to see how she's doing. This is her grandson Dean." She gave the most pleading look she could, holding her breath until the man responded.

"Dean?" the man said, turning to look at Dean, his expression softening. "She's been asking for you since she arrived." He eased the door open further and gestured for them to come in. Dean took Susie's hand as they followed the nurse. "You'll need to keep the noise down as the three other beds in her bay are occupied, but you can come in and say hi for a few minutes."

"Thank you," Dean said.

"How is she?" Susie asked.

"She's fractured her hip, and we've had to give her some pain relief, so she's a little confused."

"Will she be okay?" Dean asked, the urgency of his question making Susie squeeze his hand.

"She's booked in for surgery first thing in the morning. We can't ever make any promises," the nurse said, giving them a gentle smile. "But she's in good health, so we're optimistic. Here you are; please keep the noise down. I'll get into trouble if you wake the other patients up."

"Thank you," Susie said. Dean's focus was entirely on the small, fragile figure of his granny lying in the hospital bed, the machines around her beeping and flickering.

"I'm hoping seeing him will help her settle," the nurse said.

"Hopefully, it'll help them both," Susie said with a smile.

Dean eased himself into the chair closest to his granny's bed, reaching out to take her small hand. The fragile, crêpe texture was familiar, but no less distressing for that fact. If he could have willed some of his strength into her, he would have.

Her eyes fluttered open at the contact. "Dean," she said, her words a hoarse whisper as a smile spread across her lips. "You didn't need to come."

"As if I wasn't going to come and see what trouble you were making for the nurses."

"Hush now, boy, I'm not going to make trouble, not until after my operation anyway."

Dean blinked back tears at the easy banter that they always slipped into.

"Hello, Susie dear," Agnes said, glancing over his shoulder. "You definitely didn't need to drag that poor girl along with you."

"I wasn't going to let him have all the fun," Susie said quietly, joining in with their joking.

Grateful that whatever confusion Agnes had been experiencing earlier seemed to be gone, Dean stood and pulled another chair over for Susie to join them. "You gave us quite a scare," he said, giving his granny a mock glare.

"Oh, it's all a fuss over nothing," she said.

"You need surgery, Granny; that's a bit more than nothing."

Agnes rolled her eyes before fixing her gaze on Susie. "Arthur and Grace were here for hours earlier," she said, giving a mischievous smile. "I'm fairly sure my daughter-in-law would be sleeping on a couch somewhere in the hospital if Arthur hadn't forced her to go home. I think Susie should force you to go home too."

"I'll give you two some privacy, shall I? I'll go and check how long we can stay and find out what time the surgery is tomorrow if you like?" Susie said.

"I'm glad they were here for you," Dean said.

"You need to spend more time with your family," Agnes said, holding his gaze with her clear eyes. "Grace was beside herself when she couldn't get hold of you earlier."

Dean rubbed his head. He knew he should speak to his mum more often, but it was hard. "You know how hard it is for me to hear how amazing she thinks everyone else is."

"Grace loves you with her whole heart; whatever makes you think you're at the bottom of some imaginary list of favourites is all in your head."

"She never stops telling me how great the others are. I definitely don't imagine that, and I definitely haven't imagined how badly I let the family down," he said, knowing he was starting to sound like a stroppy teenager.

"She does that to the others about you just as much," Agnes said, squeezing his hand with surprising strength.

Dean looked up at her, blinking hard. She nodded, as though wanting to reinforce her point.

"You think you don't deserve her love, and that's the problem. It was never about Grace."

He leant back, still holding her hand but needing a little more distance.

"That's your problem with the girl too," Agnes said, nodding in the direction Susie had walked.

"Susie?" Dean asked with a frown.

"When was the last time you drove a car?" Agnes asked him, changing tack yet again.

What? Seriously, was she determined to poke at every open sore he had in one night? It was late, or stupidly early, depending on your perspective, and he wasn't in the mood for self-reflection. He just wanted to enjoy the relief of knowing his granny was going to be okay. "I killed someone," he said, the words almost whispered.

"You didn't kill anyone; you were in an accident. You're holding that woman's death over your own head, and it's time to stop," she said, squeezing his hand and making him look up to meet her gaze. "You survived that accident, but are you really living?"

Dean blinked back tears. "I can't ever be good enough to make up for that," he said, the words he'd never spoken slipping out.

"You didn't cause her death, but even if you had, you owe it to her, to yourself and to the people in your life to live the best life you can, to make the best of every opportunity, to fully live. And love."

"I've tried," he said. "I date, I've just never found anyone who thinks I'm good enough that they want to stick around."

Agnes looked towards the corridor Susie had walked down again, before giving him a meaningful look.

"Granny," Dean said, rubbing his hand over his head again. "Susie is just a friend."

"And whose fault is that?"

He frowned. "She didn't want to be more than my friend before I put her in hospital, this hospital actually. She certainly isn't going to want to now."

Agnes just studied him.

"Is she?" he asked, the question slipping out before he could stop it, the hopeful tone making his granny grin at him in a way that made him truly regret letting the words spill from his lips.

"Are you so sure of how she felt back then?"

He frowned, wondering just how deeply his forehead could wrinkle before causing some kind of permanent damage. "Don't," he said, not wanting to taunt himself with dreams he knew weren't real. "If I'm ever going to find the right person, I need it to be someone who wants me for everything I am."

"Dean, I don't like to interfere," Agnes said, and he snorted despite himself. She gave him a mock glare. "You want someone who loves you for everything you are. That girl knows every part of you, and she's here with you, in the middle of the night, just to make sure you're okay."

"She was worried about you too."

"I know, she's a good girl like that, but she's not here for me, she's here for you. If you don't want to face up to the truth of how she felt about you when you were younger, I can't make you, but I was around to see the pain she was in when you left for London."

Dean opened his mouth to interject, but she waved him into silence.

"I'm not talking about her injuries. I'm talking about the fact that girl didn't leave her house for months. Her mum was beside herself. Susie was grieving for you."

Dean swallowed. Susie had told him he'd hurt her, and in a way completely different to the way he'd been fixated on, but he'd never imagined the depth of her pain. The idea that someone as strong and determined as Susie, a woman who'd survived her dad's betrayal, had been close to breaking because of him was nearly enough to bring him to his knees.

"Don't you dare add this to your pile of things to flagellate yourself over," Agnes said. "I'm only telling you this so you don't make the same mistake again."

He nodded, not sure he could really agree with her warning, but wanting to let her know he'd heard it.

"She's clearly forgiven you. You need to decide if you're prepared to let the past go, to forgive yourself and grab the only future that I think will make you both happy." Agnes nodded in the direction Susie had gone in again, and Dean's heart pounded so loudly he was sure the entire ward would be able to hear it.

"What if it's too late?" he whispered, not meeting Agnes's eyes.

"She wouldn't be here if it was too late," she said. The words were spoken in the sort of no-nonsense tone that he recognised from years of hearing it.

CHAPTER THIRTY-THREE

Pulling up outside of the house Susie still shared with her mum, Dean realised he hadn't even walked past it in years. It was the sort of place that had rocketed in value over time with more and more people looking to enjoy living in the countryside while they commuted to work. Tucked away in the cul-de-sac of half privately owned and half council owned properties, it was somewhere easily avoided on his infrequent visits home.

Susie had quickly agreed to Dean's request to crash here rather than dropping him home for what was left of the night. He'd said he didn't want to wake whichever of his family members were in residence at his parents' house after the night they'd already had, but really he didn't think he had enough emotional strength to face any of them just yet. Hopefully, a couple of hours' sleep would be enough to rebuild his armour.

"I'll dig some blankets out for you," Susie said quietly as they slipped through the front door.

"Don't worry," Dean said. "It's too hot to need them anyway."

"*Oooff,*" Susie groaned, mirroring Dean's own groan as his toes hit something where he'd been expecting open hallway.

Susie flicked the light on, and Dean took in the piles of newspapers that were stacked haphazardly throughout the small area. Susie's face fell as she took in the sight, and she moved to the entrance to the lounge, where she flicked on another light and sighed, her shoulders falling.

Dean walked up behind her, resting his hands on her shoulders and easing her back against his chest. The furniture was covered in stacks of a myriad of things. What appeared to be partially used balls of wool fell off the armchair in the corner, and the couch had a stack of what Dean could tell was the sort of junk mail most people just threw straight into the recycling.

"I'm sorry," Susie said, pulling away from him and starting to move things, clearing the sofa that he was supposed to be sleeping on tonight.

"Why are you sorry?" he asked, frowning, and moving to help her.

She gestured around them. "I've only been gone two months. I don't know how she's managed to get things like this in such a short space of time."

"Does she do this a lot?" Dean asked, realising that Dorothy might have a real problem if this level of hoarding was only from the last two months. He remembered the house always being a little cluttered, Dorothy always having a number of things hanging around for use just in case, but this was a whole other level.

Susie nodded. "It's been worse the last few years. We agreed she'd just use the dining room, but maybe that didn't help." She straightened and headed to the dining room, pulling the door open. Dean didn't need to wait for her to put the light on to see just how crammed it was. "Damn it," she said, her head dropping into her hands. "I shouldn't have gone."

"I don't think you can help her with this," Dean said, walking over to wrap her in his arms. "Look, we're both exhausted; why don't you go to bed and you can speak to your mum in the morning to try to find out what's happening then."

"Are you sure you don't want me to drop you home?" Susie asked, giving the room a despairing look.

"I'm sure. Look, the couch is perfectly serviceable, and I'd be able to sleep in your car at this stage. This is definitely a step up from your car."

Instead of responding to his cheeky comment, she gave him a weak smile and headed upstairs.

"I'm worried about you, Mum."

Susie's voice woke Dean what felt like far too soon, but the sun blazing through the tiny gap at the top of the curtains in the lounge made it clear it was late enough. He held himself still, torn between not wanting to eavesdrop, but also not wanting to disturb what was bound to be a difficult conversation.

"I'm fine. You don't need to fuss, love," Dorothy said, her sweet tone holding an edge of determination.

"Look at the place," Susie said, her tone hopeless.

"It's fine," Dorothy said.

"Fine? It's full of literal rubbish," Susie said.

"I might need it," Dorothy said.

"Holding on to it won't bring Dad back, and even if it did, he won't be setting foot in this house again if I have anything to do with it."

"Don't bring that man up; he isn't welcome here," Dorothy said.

"Well, we agree on that one," Susie said, and Dean could hear the smile in her voice.

The sounds of hot drinks being made filled the silence for a minute.

"I'm sorry for leaving you to cope on your own, Mum," Susie said. "My placement is nearly finished, so I'll just go get my stuff and come home."

"Don't you dare cut your placement short on my account. I'm just fine," Dorothy said with a sniff and a sharpness to her tone that Dean recognised.

"I need to be here for you, Mum," Susie said. "Unless you'll go and see the counsellor I found?"

"Just because you don't agree with how I do things doesn't mean I need a counsellor," Dorothy said, the edge in her voice growing.

Susie's next words made it clear she recognised it too. "Sorry, Mum, I love you, and you know I'm happy to be here for you," she said, ending the conversation by announcing that she was off for a shower.

Dean suspected she'd simply paused the disagreement for later, rather than abandoned it completely. He waited a few minutes before shuffling around on the couch, not wanting Dorothy to be embarrassed at the idea he'd overheard their discussion.

"I'm not stupid, Dean," Dorothy said as he sat up, able to look over the back of the couch and through the hatch into the small kitchen. "I know you heard all of that."

He gave her a rueful smile. "I didn't want to interfere."

"Well, now you've heard that my daughter thinks I'm crazy," she said, her usually cheerful lips pursing.

Dean moved off the couch and padded through to the kitchen; this wasn't a conversation he wanted to have through a two-foot hole in the wall. "You know Susie loves you," he said, when he joined Dorothy in the kitchen and accepted a mug of coffee from her.

Dorothy nodded her agreement. "That doesn't mean I like her insinuating I need a psychologist."

"I know you love her too," Dean said.

"Of course, I do," Dorothy said, frowning at him. "Why would you even say that?"

"Because I think Susie is so worried about you that she'd give up the things she wants in life to give everything she can to help you," he said, keeping his words steady as he spoke, wanting to make sure he didn't get Dorothy's barriers so far up that she couldn't hear what he was saying.

"We're a team, we always have been," Dorothy said.

"You were a family. You became a team after Stanley left, and she's carried the weight of trying to fill the gap he left in your life ever since," Dean said, steeling himself to continue in the face of Dorothy's dropping expression. "Look, I know how much it means to Susie that you two are so close, and I know she would never want that to change, but do you know how hard she works, and has worked for years? Yet she still can't even afford the supplies she needs for her own artwork. I think you know why she can't afford anything for herself, and I know she wants to do it, but do you want her life to be all about you and what you want?"

"How dare you say that to me?" Dorothy asked, her eyes filling with tears. "I would never hold her back."

Dean deliberately looked across to the hatch into the lounge, and at the chaos within it before turning back to Dorothy. "As long as she's worried about you, she'll hold herself back. Are you even happy here?" he asked.

Dorothy had studied the mug in her hands for so long he'd begun to wonder if she'd ever answer him. "What do I do?" she asked, her eyes searching his face.

The irony of someone asking him for advice on how to straighten their life out wasn't lost on him, but maybe the fact he'd been letting his own past rule his life for so long meant he could at least steer Dorothy away from the approaches that he knew were definitely the wrong ones. "Try the counsellor," he said, reaching out and placing his hand over Dorothy's. He had no idea what demons she was battling, he wasn't even sure she did, but that's what the professionals were for — to help the rest of the world figure this stuff out.

Dorothy nodded her agreement just as Susie walked into the kitchen.

"Do you want to take a shower or anything before we head back to the hospital?" Susie asked.

"No, I'm good. Might as well face the horde looking as dishevelled as I feel," Dean said in a tone he knew wasn't as light as he'd been aiming for.

As they went to leave, Dorothy followed them. "Don't cut your placement short, love," she said to Susie, who turned to her mother with a frown. "I promise I'll call the counsellor first thing on Monday."

"Are you sure?" Susie asked, studying her mum.

"It's time," Dorothy said, her shoulders visibly squaring as she spoke. Dorothy turned to Dean, as though seeking approval, and he saw Susie's head swivel between the two of them before she stepped back and gave her mum a hug that brought tears to both women's eyes.

"Thank you, Mum," Susie whispered, stepping back and walking towards Dean. "What did you do?" she mouthed, but he just shrugged. He hadn't done anything except remind Dorothy of things she already knew.

"Dean," Dorothy said, beckoning him to her. He walked back up the path, and into her outstretched arms. "Thank you for looking out for my baby girl," she whispered into his ear. "But please don't hurt her again."

Dean leant back, tilting his chin down so he could meet her gaze. "I've learned my lesson there," he said seriously. "I promise you I will never hurt her again."

Dorothy gave him a smile that said she accepted he meant the words, but that made it clear he'd need to prove he could be trusted to stand by them.

CHAPTER THIRTY-FOUR

Susie had always loved the way the area looked in the summer, but driving to the hospital, she found she couldn't enjoy the way the plants running along the sides of the narrow lanes had grown, or the lush blooms that added colour to their journey. Instead, she found herself sneaking glances at Dean. Despite her pressing him, he'd refused to tell her what he'd said to her mum. She knew whatever it was must have been huge; anything less wouldn't have changed her mum's opinion about seeing a counsellor. She should know; she'd been trying to get her to do it for ages.

The hoarding had started after her dad had left, so Susie knew it was some sort of coping mechanism for her mum. At first, she'd even been stupid enough to help her with it, pleased that anything was making her mum able to function again. When the first pile of newspapers had reached shoulder height, Dorothy had actually gone back to work. Unfortunately, the ability to function outside of the house had simply escalated her new habit.

"It isn't always that bad," Susie said, not wanting Dean to judge her mum too harshly.

"I'm assuming it's better when you're there to look after her and keep some control," he said, giving her a gentle smile.

She nodded. "I really shouldn't have left her. I really did think she was doing better," she said with a sigh.

"You can't be her parent forever," Dean said softly.

"I can't abandon her either," she said, trying not to blush at the realisation she kept talking about things that reminded them both of the fact that was exactly what Dean had done to her.

"With any luck, the counsellor will help," Dean said.

They arrived at the hospital with just enough time to give Agnes a quick hug before she was wheeled away on a gurney for her operation. The Parker family had assembled en masse, and it seemed Grace was letting the presence of all of her sons distract her from her worry about her mother-in-law.

"Mrs Parker will be in surgery for a couple of hours," the bemused nurse said, taking in the assembled family. "It'll be tricky having the family room full for all that time, so why don't you head back to the coffee shop for a bit?"

Susie smiled at the nurse's attempt at tactfully telling them to go away. It was clear the hospital wasn't equipped for this number of people to hang around for one patient, but none of the Parker clan were prepared to leave completely.

By the time they'd navigated the endless corridors to find the coffee shop and all ordered and received their drinks, the best part of half an hour had passed.

Susie found herself between Dean and Maggie. Nathan, Chris and Joe were sitting opposite them and Grace, looking as fragile as her mother-in-law, was sitting slightly apart with Dean's dad, Arthur, who simply held her hand as she stared into the distance.

"So, how are the wedding plans going?" Susie asked Maggie.

"They aren't really," Maggie said, wrinkling her nose. "We'll figure it out, but we're both so focused on the renovations that we haven't even set a date yet."

"Not getting cold feet, are you?" Susie asked, teasing.

"Not at all," Maggie said, her adoration for her fiancé obvious as she met his gaze. "The actual wedding just doesn't feel that important."

Susie smiled, pleased things were going so well for her friends.

"Anyway," Maggie said, leaning closer and lowering her voice as the men returned to their debate about the performance of the village cricket team. "What about you and Dean? What's going on there?"

Susie frowned at her. "What do you mean?"

"You're here together." Maggie gave her a questioning look as she lifted her coffee.

"It was too late to get a train when he picked up Grace's message last night, so I gave him a lift," Susie said with a shrug.

"And he's been glued to your side since you got here, because…?"

"Because I'm his friend and he's worried about his granny; you know how close the two of them are," Susie said, taking a sip of her own coffee, and resisting the urge to glance at Dean and see if he'd heard Maggie's hushed comments, and if so, how he was reacting to them.

"So, you're trying to tell me it's all innocent? That you haven't so much as kissed?"

Susie felt the heat in her cheeks. Her mind flashed back to the sensation of Dean's lips on hers the night she'd shared the news of her show with him. That was two weeks ago. Given that nothing had happened since, it clearly hadn't meant anything romantic. Her gaze darted to Dean, worried he would pick up on the whispered conversation, and her own confusion over it.

"Fine, I won't push," Maggie said. Susie let out a sigh of relief, until Maggie added, "For now."

Fine, she probably needed to talk to someone about her confused feelings for Dean, but she definitely didn't want to do it when the man in question was right there.

"God, if Mum tells me how amazing your career is one more time, I swear I'll throttle you, but as you're never here I might be tempted to throttle her instead," Joe said, jabbing his finger at Dean.

Dean gave his brother a gloating smile that he didn't feel. He knew just how much his mum adored Joe; as the baby of the family he was coddled, and despite the fact he was currently trying his hand at carpentry with Nathan, Dean had lost track of how many careers the lad had been certain were the perfect one for him before dropping them months later for the next new and shiny thing.

The fact Grace was constantly singing Joe's praises when he couldn't hold down a job for more than a few months at a time grated on his nerves. At twenty-three, Joe really ought to have sorted himself out more by now.

"Don't even try it," Chris said, nudging the youngest Parker brother. "You think we don't get sick of hearing how great you're going to be at whatever flavour of the month job you're trying out now?"

"Well, at least hearing how perfect you, Paula and baby Oliver are is just about bearable," Dean said with a roll of his eyes at Chris.

"You'd think she'd have sussed out that none of us want to hear how brilliant each other are by now," Chris said.

"She's proud of you all, and you know it's her way of keeping you up to date with each other's news," Paula said, coming up behind her husband and handing Oliver to him. "I can't get him to settle; you need to work your magic."

Chris stood up and rocked his son in his arms, the mewling cries subsiding almost instantly.

"I'll never work out how you can do that and I can't," Paula said, taking a bite of Chris's half-eaten chocolate muffin.

"Hey," Chris said to his wife. "You said you didn't want a cake."

"I didn't," Paula said, giving her husband a smile as she continued eating the treat.

"And don't get me started on how much she talks about Nathan," Joe said, continuing their conversation as though Paula hadn't spoken at all.

Dean gave him a questioning look.

"You can't tell me you don't get it as well," Joe said, giving Nathan a sideways look. "'Nathan's so talented; he can make anything. Maggie's so amazing; they are going to be so happy together. I can't wait to start planning the wedding. I bet Nathan makes a great father.' Honestly," Joe said, "if I never have to hear about you lot again, it'll be too soon."

"Come on," Nathan said. "It's not like I don't get it too. Mum hasn't shut up about how great it is that Dean got promoted to senior developer, and that was three years ago. She doesn't even say hi when I answer the phone, just launches straight into it."

Dean felt his frown deepen as he absorbed the exchange between his brothers. Listening to the others, he began to question how his conversations with Grace made him feel. Agnes's words from the night before shoved themselves to the front of his mind. Could he have been taking his mum's approach to all of her sons too personally? Reacting as though they were some intended slight, instead of just the way she spoke about them all to each other?

Before he could investigate his feelings any more, Grace came over to gather them all up so they could go and see how their granny had fared through her surgery.

Relieved that Agnes's surgery had gone well, the family were louder than usual. Dean took a deep breath, letting his nerves settle. Glancing at his watch, he realised it was nearly lunchtime.

Walking over to Susie, he positioned himself between her and Maggie, his back to Maggie so she wouldn't hear what he was saying.

"If you don't head back soon, you're going to miss your show," Dean said quietly to Susie, catching her before Maggie could claim her attention again. He wanted to let her know how finely she was cutting it while respecting her decision not to tell anyone else about the show.

Susie glanced at her phone, her face dropping as she saw the time and realised he was right. "Are you coming back?" she asked.

"Do you want me to?" Dean held his breath, nervous at being rejected, but also nervous about just how much would change if she said yes.

Susie studied her shoes; she was wearing the trainers he'd quickly come to learn were her favourites. They were well worn, and the orange trim was barely visible in some places, but they were the ones she seemed to default to. "I'd understand if you wanted to stay here," she said eventually.

Dean swallowed, determined not to be weak again; this time he was going to face her, even when he was afraid of what she was going to say. "Do you want me to come with you?"

Susie nodded and he let out a relieved breath. "I'd like you to be with me at my show," she said, before hurriedly carrying on. "But I understand if you want to stay here with your granny. I could stay with you."

At her words Dean wanted nothing more than to wrap her in his arms and hold her there forever. The idea that she'd even consider giving up something she'd worked so hard for, something that could be the start of her dreams, filled him with a warmth that he didn't think he'd ever experienced before. Instead, he kept his arms firmly at his sides, not wanting to deal with the inevitable questions from his family, especially when he didn't have any idea what the answers were. "There is no way I'd let you miss tonight," he said, giving her a small smile. "Let's just say goodbye to Granny and we can get out of here, together."

CHAPTER THIRTY-FIVE

They had barely had enough time to get to Dean's flat, change and get to the show before the doors were opened to let the evening's guests start entering, but Dean found he couldn't move.

After saying her hellos to Sam and Edwina, and giving them her profuse apologies for abandoning them the night before and her heartfelt thanks for the chance they were taking on her work, on her, Susie had led Dean through the gallery space. She'd said she wanted to take the opportunity to enjoy the work before she had to start chatting to the art connoisseurs who would be attending this evening. They'd started walking around and Susie had explained that she wanted to look at Sam's work before going to the corner where she'd started helping Sam and Edwina set her work up.

However, they'd only made it around halfway around when Susie had stopped abruptly. Following her gaze with his own, Dean took in the sight of an image that wasn't of any specific object, but that seemed to call to his very soul. The piece seemed to be made up of layers of colour. The surface was all faded colours and curling edges, as though the paint was drying out and flaking away, but visible through the cracks was a different story. Rich jewel colours peeked through, as though it was something ancient and private. The painting's layers slowly peeled back, allowing its true glory to be revealed to all who came near.

"I can't believe they put it here," Susie breathed.

Glancing around, Dean registered that the piece was on one of the broad white pillars that formed a kind of rotunda in the centre of the room. As Susie's words sank in, he read the little plaque beneath the painting, seeing her name in the curled font. "It's incredible," he said, smiling at her.

"You inspired me," she said, blushing slightly and dropping her gaze. "I couldn't have created this if it wasn't for you."

He turned his gaze back to the image, feeling the emotion that Susie had poured into it. He was aware of her, waiting for his reaction to the fact he'd played any part in the creation.

"Pleased?" Sam asked, his focus on Susie as he approached them.

"I can't believe you've put it here," Susie said. "Surely you should save the best spots for your own work."

"The best spots go to the best work," Sam said. "You've finally let all of your feelings feed your work, and it shows. This is the most incredible thing I've seen in years."

Dean smiled as Susie gave Sam a hug, but he couldn't take his eyes off the image. It was only when Susie touched his arm that he pulled his gaze away.

"I have to go and circulate a bit," she said, her face wrinkling in apology.

"Of course, go and be adored," he said, giving her a smile. "You deserve it."

Susie rolled her eyes and turned to move towards the area of the gallery where her other pieces were displayed.

"You're wrong, you know," Dean said, causing her to turn back to him. Once he was sure he had her attention, he continued, "I didn't have any part in this." He gestured to the piece that had captivated him so fully. "This is all you."

The pink of her cheeks deepened, and she gave him a smile before heading away again.

Dean meant every word of it, though; whatever part she thought he'd played, this was a culmination of her hard work and her talent. He finally turned his back on the artwork and watched the woman who had captivated him make her way around the room, chatting to everyone as she did, leaving smiles and joy in her wake.

Turning back to the image, he took a deep breath. The work seemed to speak to his soul, as though encouraging him to pull back his own layers, coaxing him to go back to a time when he wasn't buried under the tarnish of the last few years. Back to a time when he could fully be himself.

Smiling at Charles and Laura, who came up to admire the work, he chatted to them about their own progress during their placement with Sam. He was pleased to find that the pair were incredibly positive about the whole thing, despite their own work not getting chosen.

Watching Edwina discreetly place the little red sold sticker under the piece, Dean felt a pang of regret. He hadn't been able to move away from it all evening, so much so that he'd been tempted to buy it for himself. He'd stopped himself from doing just that at the realisation that Susie would never have believed he'd bought it because he'd truly wanted it. He didn't want to take away the joy of her first professional sales, and some part of him understood she'd always wonder if he'd just bought it because he was her friend, or worse, to make up for his guilt over leaving her behind. Now though, he was regretting his decision.

CHAPTER THIRTY-SIX

Taking in the small red dots that sat beneath each of her pieces, Susie felt the grin stretching her cheeks. "I can't believe they've all sold," she said.

"I can," Dean said. When she gave him a questioning look, he continued, "They are amazing; you are incredibly talented."

Susie slipped her hand into his at the sincerity in his words.

"Looks like I might need you to teach me some things," Sam said, smiling at her in genuine delight over her success. "Congratulations."

"Thank you so much, for everything," Susie said, not knowing how to express just how much she appreciated what he had done for her.

"It's my pleasure," Sam said. "I know your placement is over, but it would be nice to keep in touch?"

Susie nodded. "I'd love that."

"Right, I need to go and speak to Edwina about the sales. Why don't you two take off? It's been a long day."

Susie nodded and let Dean lead her out of the gallery. Outside, the evening was humid, as though threatening a storm.

"I've had a couple of glasses of champagne, so I'd better leave the car here," Susie said.

"I'll call us an Uber," Dean said.

"That's a waste of money when the Tube station is only a couple of streets away," she said, smiling at him and dragging him in that direction before he could object.

After swiping their Oyster cards, they made their way down to the almost deserted platform.

"It's strange seeing it so empty," Susie said, looking around.

"It'll get busier as we cross the centre of the city," Dean said, wrapping his arm around her shoulders.

"Thank you for coming back with me today," Susie said.

"Thank you for wanting me to be there with you," Dean said, his gaze dropping to her lips.

Before she could question herself too deeply, Susie stretched onto her toes and, leaning closer to Dean, pressed her lips to his.

For a beat, she wondered if she'd made a huge mistake; his entire frame seemed frozen rigid. Just as she resigned herself to stepping back and attempting to make him believe it had been nothing more than a friendly gesture, his arms wound around her back, his mouth softening.

She let out an involuntary moan at the sensation. She'd fought hard against dreams of kissing Dean when they were younger, certain that romance didn't last, and determined not to let anything spoil their friendship. Realising that her father's behaviour wasn't a predictor for all relationships hadn't made her any better at choosing a partner, though, so finding herself here, years later, actually kissing Dean was like she'd wished her dreams into reality.

As he pulled her body against his solid frame, the rumble of an approaching train caused her to step back. The *whoosh* of hot air pushed through the station by the train wrapped around them both like a cocoon. Without taking his arms from her waist, Dean rested his forehead on hers, holding her gaze with his.

"I'd like to do that again," he said softly.

Unable to find the words, Susie nodded.

Once they were on the train, seated side by side, Dean laced his fingers through hers, his thumb brushing the sensitive inside of her wrist. Watching his reflection in the window on the opposite side of the carriage, she realised that simply holding hands with Dean was more charged than any of the encounters she'd had over recent years. None of the men she'd dated had created this sort of response in her. It left her feeling restless and needy. Her foot tapped as she willed the journey to be done, though she was afraid the magical bubble would burst as soon as they arrived.

After a line change, they finally emerged out into the night, and this time it didn't provide any relief from the sticky heat of the underground. The threatening storm seemed to be closer than when they'd entered the station near the gallery.

Silently, they walked from the station back to Dean's flat side by side, the hum of traffic that never seemed to stop in the city mingling with the occasional holler of people enjoying the humid night. Susie didn't dare reach out and touch Dean's hand again, knowing that any kind of contact was going to cause the sort of response she wouldn't have any control over. Despite the fact he seemed to want her as much as she wanted him, she had no indication of whether it was a reaction to the events of the last twenty-four hours, and something that would be cause for regret, or whether it was a sign he wanted their relationship to change permanently.

When they were a street away from his flat, a rumble of thunder rippled around them, the sound seeming to echo through the quiet streets. Almost as soon as it faded, fat drops of rain began to fall, soaking them within seconds. The instant drop in temperature seemed to ease the tension that had been building between them and they turned to each other with a laugh before picking up the pace and running the last of the distance to Dean's flat. Trudging up the stairs, they let the water drip onto the carpet, grinning as they made their way up to the third floor.

As soon as Dean had let them in and the door swung closed behind them, he removed his shoes and pulled his shirt off. "I'll grab us both towels," he said.

Her entire focus on the play of muscles in his bare back, Susie found herself unable to respond. He turned to face her, and she found herself equally captivated by his chest, her eyes drifting down to where the light smattering of hair led into his trousers.

"Susie," Dean said, his voice low and hoarse.

She looked up to meet his heated gaze and swallowed at the need that greeted her.

"Can I kiss you?" he asked, his voice almost breaking on the words.

She nodded, wanting to feel his lips on her so much that any concern about the future was just a shadow in the back of her mind — a shadow dispelled by the light in Dean's eyes at her consent.

He stopped with mere inches between them, raising his hands and burying them in her short hair.

She swallowed and Dean finally lowered his head, his lips meeting hers, the contact soft and delicate. Parting her lips, she encouraged him to deepen the kiss. As one hand slid down her back, she arched into him, and his answering groan seemed to light something in them both, the gentle, tender start quickly vanishing in a gasp of urgency.

Dean's hands slid to the bottom of her top, and bunching it up, he leant back, his lips leaving hers just long enough to lift it over her head and discard it.

His lips travelled down her neck, over the small curve of her breast and down her stomach, and every inch of her felt as though it was being worshipped as he went. Reaching the line where her jeans met her hip bones, he popped the buttons open, and they both laughed as the saturated fabric resisted his efforts at removing them.

"Nice pants," he said, glancing up to give her a wink.

Susie closed her eyes and groaned; she didn't own anything resembling fancy underwear. She quickly forgot about her embarrassment as his lips brushed the top edge of the fabric. Her jeans finally gave up the fight and began to shift down her legs. His lips tracing their movement, Dean kissed the top of her legs, and then stopped, falling back on his heels, his expression one of horror.

Flinching, Susie pushed his hand off her hip and attempted to pull the jeans back up, a familiar but unwelcome heat washing through her at his response. She'd long grown used to the scar that spanned the top half of her left thigh; she was even used to the way new lovers responded to it. She usually prepared them for it before starting, just because she hated when their shock interrupted her libido. She'd been so caught up in the moment with Dean that she hadn't thought to stop and explain, and even if she had, she'd have assumed he knew about it.

"Susie," he said, her name just a breath from his lips.

"It's fine, I get it," she said, eyes scanning for her abandoned top so she could escape to the sanctuary of her room, anything to get away from the way he was looking at her.

"I'm so sorry," he said, his head dropping to the ground.

"It's fine," she said. "I get that it's not exactly appealing." There, her top had ended up behind the small unit Dean used for keys and post. She moved, determined to grab it and get away, to put distance between her and this humiliation.

Dean's head snapped up, and his brow furrowed as his hand shot out and grabbed her wrist. "You think I don't want you anymore, because of your scar?"

Susie blinked hard, the heat building in her eyes letting her know she had moments to get out of there before she gave away just how much his reaction hurt.

"Susie," he said, dropping her arm. "I don't deserve you."

She rolled her eyes, welcome anger taking the place of her self-pity. "Don't hide behind platitudes," she said, knowing her abrupt shift of emotion was clear in her tone. "At least have the courtesy to admit it's off-putting."

Rising to his feet, Dean stepped closer, forcing her to look up at him. "There is nothing, not one single thing about you that makes me want you any less," he said, holding her gaze. "But I put that there." He jabbed his finger at her thigh. "Or are you going to try to pretend you were in some other accident that caused this much damage to your leg?"

Susie shook her head, her anger bleeding out at the realisation his reaction, the disgust, had been aimed at himself.

"I'm sorry," he whispered, dropping to his knees in front of her, his head bowed. "How can you ever forgive me?"

Sucking in a breath, she studied his still figure, trying to work out how to put into words the way she felt about him, about their complex history. "Dean," she said, finally speaking as she dropped to her own knees. Placing her hand under his chin, she eased his face up, forcing him to look at her. "You saved my life that night. I don't know how many ways I can tell you that you don't need my forgiveness," she said, her voice breaking. "The only forgiveness you need is your own."

Dean's head dropped again at her final words, but not before she saw the tears that had begun to track down his face. "I don't deserve you," he said, reaching for her without looking up.

Susie allowed him to pull her close, his lips peppering kisses across her face before settling on her lips once more. Her hands ran down his bare back, revelling in the feel of his muscles responding to her touch. He lifted her up, encouraging her to wrap her legs around his waist, and carried her to his bedroom. Easing her onto the bed, he slowly lowered himself to her side, his hand stroking her cheek with reverence before their lips met again. Almost instantly the gentle touches vanished again, deepening into something that seemed to radiate with a mutual need.

CHAPTER THIRTY-SEVEN

Swinging the door to his flat open, Dean juggled the armful of flowers he'd collected on his way home as he tried to pull his key back out of the lock.

The joy of having Susie to come home to, to have her as the kind of partner in his life he'd always wanted, seemed to make everything in his life better. He even seemed to be impressing the partners with his newfound joy. His enthusiasm for life in general was rubbing off on all of his interactions. He knew that Susie was going to have to head home to complete her degree at the end of the summer, but he was hoping to persuade her to make her return a temporary one. They'd spent eight years apart; he could cope with the eight months it would take her to complete her final year. Besides, last time they'd been apart, it had been a complete end to any contact, something he knew was entirely his fault. This time he'd be able to visit her, and he was hoping to persuade her to do the same when she had time.

Quietly making his way to her studio, he stood in the doorway, soaking in the sight of the woman he loved pouring her heart and soul into her work. She was so absorbed in her creation that she didn't register his presence for a few minutes. When she jolted upright, her hand flying to her heart at the realisation she wasn't alone, he gave her a broad smile.

"Fancy dinner with Sam and Marina tonight?" he asked.

"That would be great, but I have a shift at Mojo later," she said. "Someone called in sick and Li Jun knows I'm always up for the extra work."

Dean wrinkled his nose; he'd wanted to arrange a nice evening for them, but she seemed to be working more shifts at the bar and the coffee shop now she'd finished her placement than she had been before.

"You already do loads of shifts," he said. "I was hoping to have a nice evening together." His good mood shifted downwards in frustration that she was putting earning a few measly extra quid ahead of them spending time together.

"I know," she said, coming over to him. "I'm sorry."

"You know you don't need to worry about money," he said.

Susie frowned back at him. "I have bills to pay," she said, the words coming out lightly despite the fact he knew they were seconds away from rehashing the one issue that seemed to cast a shadow over their newfound happiness. She'd been very clear that she wasn't about to let herself become financially dependent on a man. And even if she wanted to go with his repeated suggestion to do just that, she was funding the house she shared with her mum, and that wasn't something she'd let anyone else get sucked into.

"Well, let's have breakfast together instead," he suggested, his heart plummeting when his words made her wince.

"I'm really sorry. I told Momin and Zara that I'd cover for them at Ground Up in the morning," she said.

"But you don't usually work Thursday mornings," Dean said, aware that his tone was edging towards whingeing, but unable to stop himself.

"I know, but they asked because they want to go to their daughter's school assembly. Apparently, she's getting some kind of award." Before Dean could open his mouth, Susie continued, "Are those for me?" She gestured to the bundles in his arms.

Glad of the reprieve from what he knew was going to turn into an argument, he gave her a smile and shoved the bouquet of giant daisies towards her. "They made me think of you," he said. They were obviously a good choice, because any sign of frustration vanished from her face.

"You're an idiot," she said, but there was no heat in her words. "But I love them, thank you."

She reached up to kiss him. The action was far too brief for his liking, but he followed her as she headed out to the kitchen.

"Do you even own a vase?" she asked.

Dean frowned, realising the flaw in his grand gesture. With a shrug he let her know he didn't own one.

Undeterred, Susie pulled a collection of pint glasses from the cupboard and began to arrange the flowers into small bunches. Once she was done, she set them out on every surface in the lounge and kitchen area of the flat. "They are gorgeous," she said, standing back to admire the room once she was finished.

"You are gorgeous," Dean corrected, resting his chin on her head as he embraced her from behind, easing her back against his chest, the contact settling something deep inside of him.

"I'm not working tomorrow," she said, and he felt the last of his tension drain away. She wanted to spend time with him.

He understood that she was used to taking care of herself; it was going to take time for her to realise they were a team now, that they could take care of each other. It didn't mean that she wasn't making him a priority in her life. He couldn't let his insecurities screw this up. He had to hang on to the fact that she had chosen to be with him, and that was the first time someone who knew everything about him, the good and the bad, had made that choice.

CHAPTER THIRTY-EIGHT

Pulling her bag over her shoulder, Susie rooted around for the phone that was ringing. Stepping to the side so she'd be out of the flow of people heading for the underground, she frowned at the number flashing on her screen. The area code was from back home, but she had everyone's number saved.

"Hello," she said, answering the call.

"Hello, is Mrs Lucas there?" a female voice asked.

"This is her daughter; can I help?" Susie asked, a spike of anxiety worming into her chest.

"We were expecting Mrs Lucas for an appointment this morning and she didn't attend; we were calling to check everything was okay and to see if she wanted to reschedule."

Susie's heart sank; the only place she could think of where her mum had an appointment, that would have her contact number, was the therapist Dorothy had promised she'd go to see.

"Is that the Honeyford Counselling Services?" Susie asked.

"Yes," the woman replied.

"Can we get back to you to reschedule?" she asked. "I'll need to check with Mum when works for her."

"Of course," the woman said. "Just give us a call."

Ending the call, Susie leant against the brick wall of the Tube station entrance. Her mum hadn't gone for the appointment. She'd been so sure she was going to attend this time. That's what she got for thinking things might start going her way.

"You'll never believe what I managed today," Dean said, appearing in the doorway, his lips curling with amusement.

"What?" Susie asked, enjoying the sight of the man she loved in such a good mood.

"What's going on?" he asked, looking around, his expression dropping.

Glancing around the room, Susie realised he wasn't asking what she was doing; after all, anyone with eyes could see the half-packed suitcases on the bed and know what she was doing. He wanted to know why. Rubbing her face, she sighed. "Mum missed her appointment with the counsellor," she said.

"I got us tickets to the Shakespeare performance in Regent's Park tonight."

She stepped over the rucksack on the floor and slipped her arms around his waist. "I'm sorry, that would have been amazing," she said with genuine regret.

"So, you're still going?" Dean asked, stepping back and out of her arms.

"I don't have a choice," Susie said. "You saw how bad Mum was. I can't leave her on her own."

"But you can leave me?" he asked.

"I'm not leaving you," she said. "It's not like we're splitting, up; we just won't be living together."

"You're leaving me."

"We knew I was going to have to go home soon," she said. "I have to be back in time for the new academic year."

"That was about finishing your studies; this is about putting other people ahead of our relationship."

Susie flinched, as though the words had been a physical hit. "You could come with me," she said.

"My job is here," Dean said, rubbing his head, as though confused she'd even suggest it.

"A job you hate," she said.

"I could be a partner soon."

"Another job you don't really want," she said, holding his gaze.

"Look, if I don't make partner, maybe I could consider moving back home," he said with a shrug.

Susie threw her hands in the air. "You're giving me a hard time about prioritising my mum's mental wellbeing, but you're prioritising a job you might not get, and even if you do, I don't think you really want it. Can you hear how unfair that is?" She threw a couple of T-shirts into one of her cases, giving up on trying to fold things neatly. "I don't expect you to walk away from your life just to be with me. I actually thought we could make this work by being ourselves."

"And what is that supposed to mean?"

"Why don't we face the fact this isn't going to work?" Susie said, turning her back on Dean and focusing on fitting her jeans into her larger suitcase, trying to avoid tripping over Liquorice as she did. Oh God, was she really thinking about ending things with Dean? She'd truly believed all her dreams had come true. Unfortunately, she had to accept that it was going to take both of them to keep those dreams fixed in reality, and Dean didn't seem to understand that.

"What?" Dean said, shock clear in his tone as he took a step towards her.

Susie forced herself to face him and hold his gaze. "You need to get to a place where you're comfortable with who you are, and what you want," she said. "Because until you are, I don't think you can accept me for who I am: someone who will always look out for the people I love, all of them."

"So that's it, we're over? Just like that?" He rubbed his head with both his hands, his agitation threatening to break her resolve.

"Dean," she said. "I want us to be together. I want us to have a future together."

His face lightened at her words and he took another step towards her.

She held up her hand to stop his movement. "But that's not going to happen until you're happy with yourself, until you've truly forgiven yourself for the accident and accepted that you, just as you are, are good enough," she said.

"Who I am isn't good enough," he said. "Because if it was, you'd be staying."

"I'm sorry, Dean," she said, a pain radiating through her chest that she hadn't experienced since she was twenty-one and he'd walked away from her. "But until you accept yourself, you're always going to need someone else to give you the confidence and certainty about your place in the world, and that's not a good way to build a partnership."

"I'm sorry I can't just snap my fingers and make everything the way you want it," Dean said, his lip curling unpleasantly, "but as you say, wishes don't make dreams come true."

Liquorice wound around Susie's legs, as though seeking comfort from the sudden change in mood. Oh, she was going to miss the kitten. Taking a deep breath, she steadied herself.

"It's not about what I want; it's about what we both deserve," she said, blinking back the heat in her eyes. "I can't make you see your own worth; no one can do that for you. You need to face your own demons before you're ready to be with someone else."

"You don't want me." His words were flat, not a question.

"I love you, Dean," she said. "But I can't be your crutch. I deserve someone who is with me because they want to be, not because I plug some missing piece of their own self-worth."

"That's not what this is about," he said, gesturing between them.

"No? Then what is it about?" she asked.

"The fact you're running home the second something isn't going smoothly, when I'm standing here telling you I need you, makes it very clear what it's about," he said, his tone sharp.

"No, it doesn't. You know how vulnerable my mum is; you saw how bad things were." Susie sucked in a breath, trying to gather her thoughts when her heart was pounding so hard in her chest she thought it might break through. She forced herself to meet his gaze. "You want me to stay so you feel like you're the most important person in my life. That's not how love works, Dean."

"Yes, it is," Dean said.

Susie turned to look out the window, taking in the heat of the day, the bright sunshine at odds with how she felt; it was as though every emotion she had was rubbed raw and pulled outside of her, exposed for the world to see. "I love you, Dean, but loving someone doesn't mean stopping caring for and looking out for everyone else in your life. I hope you'll figure out how amazing you are for yourself, and I hope you'll come and find me when you do." She gave him a gentle smile. "But you need to do it for yourself, and I think you need to do it by yourself."

CHAPTER THIRTY-NINE

Sitting at his desk, Dean tried to summon up enough enthusiasm about the upcoming product launch to at least give the impression he cared. It had been four days since Susie had left, and it wasn't getting any easier.

"You can't call me here." Niall's voice drifted over the partition that separated their desks.

Dean's ears pricked at the unusual panic in Niall's voice. He didn't think he'd ever heard his colleague sound anything other than smug or annoyed.

"I can't get you a job right now," Niall continued. "I'll do what I can when I can."

Silence again as the caller on the other end responded to Niall's statement.

"I know you helped, and as soon as I can, I'll bring you on board like we agreed."

As Niall paused again, Dean found himself leaning closer to the partition.

"You go around telling people you solved that, and you can kiss any chance at a job goodbye." Niall's tone shifted into angry menace.

At the realisation Niall had finished his call, Dean jerked his body back, attempting to look like someone so engrossed in what they were working on that there was no way they'd have heard anything anyone else might have been saying.

Niall's head popped up over the divider. "Do you want a coffee?" he asked. "I thought I'd make a run down to Ground Up."

Dean blinked, as though just registering that Niall was talking to him and nodded. As he watched his colleague head off on an uncharacteristic drinks run, he let the thought that Niall hadn't been the one solving the coding problems roll around his brain. It would explain how all of his breakthroughs had come when he hadn't been at work. Dean considered it for a moment longer before sighing and turning back to his screen. It turned out he really didn't care.

"What's got into you?" Alex asked, dumping a pile of papers onto Dean's desk.

He looked up, frowning at the other man. The man who'd had Susie's lips on his as well. The fact she hadn't felt anything and had backed away from a relationship with him seemed scant consolation as he studied Alex.

"You've been like a bear with a sore head the last few days," Alex said, ignoring the way Dean was scowling at him.

"I'm fine," he said, determined to put an end to the conversation.

Susie thought he needed to face up to his own demons. Well, he'd show her he was more than capable of doing things without her. Picking up the phone, Dean made an appointment for that evening, determined to do something tangible to prove he didn't need anyone.

Sitting behind the wheel, Dean sucked breaths in and out through his teeth, attempting to quell the nausea that was roiling in his stomach.

"I take it you haven't driven for a while?" the sales rep from the showroom asked as Dean attempted to calm his thoughts enough to turn the key in the ignition.

The lad couldn't have been more than twenty, and rationally, Dean knew he was being pleasant enough and just making conversation, but he fought against the urge to snap at him. It was bloody obvious he hadn't driven for a long time. He had arrived at the showroom full of bluster and determination to drive, but now it was coming down to it, he didn't know if he could do it, and the realisation was making him face the fact that Susie had been right. He had to deal with his own issues before he could hope to create a strong and positive relationship with someone else, not that he could imagine doing that with anyone but Susie.

"I hope you don't think I'm overstepping," the lad said, "but my mum had trouble driving after someone crashed into her. I'm not saying you're in the same situation, but I can give you the details of the driving instructor who helped her get on the road again if you'd like."

Dean nodded. He had to face the fact he wasn't going to be able to get over this himself; he needed help. The realisation hit him that he'd been behaving exactly the same as Susie's mum, expecting her to be his crutch. The fact he'd been such a hypocrite, speaking to Dorothy about needing to get professional help instead of leaning on Susie for the rest of her life, when he was clearly attempting to do the same, made his already churning stomach roil even more.

After messaging the driving instructor — he'd been unable to face speaking to the woman — he realised that he needed to face up to more than just driving and emailed a local counselling practice. Having set up two appointments that made him nauseous just thinking about them, he decided to get roaring drunk.

Halfway through a bottle of whisky, oblivion was still evading him. As he slumped on his couch, unable to look at his home without seeing the Susie-shaped hole, Liquorice started rubbing against his ankle. As he scooped her up, she nestled into his chest and purred at the attention.

"At least I still have you," he said, swigging from the bottle again.

Sitting in front of Elizabeth and Dipesh, the two senior partners, waiting for them to finally get to the point about who they had chosen to be the new partner, Dean couldn't make himself focus on what they were saying. Forty-one — the number kept circling around his head. It had been forty-one days since Susie had walked out on him. Since he'd let her walk away from what they had together. Somehow, he'd felt every moment of those forty-one days in a way he hadn't felt the time apart for the years that had preceded her re-entering his life. He knew now that a big part of that was because in the years before, he hadn't let himself think about her. He'd forced his thoughts to anything other than the woman he'd hurt, and then abandoned.

"We feel there has been a real change in you recently," Elizabeth said.

"Yes, a sense of maturity that we haven't seen before," Dipesh added.

Dean knew he should be giving the pair his full attention, but as he made the effort to stop thinking about Susie, his thoughts drifted to his mother, in the same way they had done for the last few weeks. He'd finally taken the advice he'd been so quick to dole out and spoken to a counsellor. The few sessions he'd had with the woman had been enough to make him realise he didn't have the sort of issues that had translated themselves into any kind of medical condition, but she had forced him to take a long, detached look at the way he'd been living his life.

"So, we felt this would be a good time to talk to you about our decision on the partnership," Elizabeth said.

Dean turned his attention to the two people he was sitting in the glossy meeting room with. This was the news he'd been waiting for. He'd been so desperate for them to make a decision, but now, all he could hear were Susie's words when she accused him of choosing the possibility of a job he didn't really want over their relationship, despite the fact he knew she'd never have asked him to make that kind of choice. He knew she'd have fully supported him staying and had just thrown the words at him in retaliation for his ugly behaviour when she'd been scared for her mum. In that moment, he realised how right she had been; he didn't care about the job. He'd been so caught up in impressing his parents that he'd lost sight of what he actually wanted. The thought that he'd been so awful to Susie when he should have been supporting her sent a wave of cold guilt washing through him.

"Actually," he said, his speech slow as he tested the thoughts out at the same time as speaking them, "I'd like to withdraw from consideration."

The pair opposite him blinked, turning to look at each other before turning back to him in unison. Before they could speak, he continued, feeling more certain now.

"I'd also like to tender my resignation, with immediate effect," he said, standing as he spoke.

"That's, but, you, but…" Elizabeth said, stumbling over her words.

"I know it seems sudden to you," Dean said. "And I'll always look back on my time here fondly, but I think it's time."

"We were about to give you the partnership," Dipesh spluttered, clearly unable to understand that Dean could be doing this.

"Thank you, I'm honoured that you felt I was suitable, but it's not for me."

"What are you going to do?" Elizabeth asked, recovering more quickly than Dipesh.

"I don't know," Dean said, realising that for the first time in years, whatever he did it was going to be what he wanted, not what he thought he should want.

CHAPTER FORTY

Pushing the door open, Dean took a deep breath; it had been so long since he'd been back here without the niggle of resentment, that its absence made the whole place feel new and different. Walking through the hallway, he followed the sound of voices to the kitchen. Finding Grace and Agnes sitting together, sipping tea and eating something freshly baked, his heart swelled. He loved these women, and the reassurance of seeing them together seemed to ease another piece of his soul back into place.

Agnes looked up, studying him intently before nodding. "I need a wee," she said.

"I swear you're the only adult I know who announces when they are going to the toilet," Grace said, her head still bent over her crossword puzzle.

Agnes stood and shuffled out of the room. Dean was glad to see her up and about, but there was a stiffness to her movements that hadn't been there before. He hoped it was simply a sign that she was still healing, and not an indication of permanent deterioration. She was in her eighties, so he knew she was going to slow down and eventually stop, but he didn't want to face that yet.

"Mum," Dean said quietly when his granny had disappeared into the lounge, patting his arm as she went. She would give him as much time as he needed with his mother.

Grace's head snapped up. "Dean," she said, standing to greet him. "I didn't realise you were coming today. Is everything okay? You didn't call; we could have picked you up from the station."

He crossed the kitchen and wrapped his arms around her, holding on for a beat longer than he would have usually done, needing to feel the connection to her. "I drove," he said, stepping back.

At his words, Grace's expression froze. "You drove?" she said, when he'd begun to think she wouldn't respond to his statement.

Dean nodded, not sure what else to say.

She sank back into her chair, her hand reaching for his. "I didn't think you'd ever drive again," she said, her eyes searching his face, as though looking for some secret to unravel.

He thought he'd done a good job of hiding his motives for not driving, and for a second, he wanted to snap back at the judgement, at the hint he shouldn't have driven again, that he didn't deserve to, but he forced himself to really look at her. Her expression was one of wonder and relief, not judgement. Just how much had he misread over the years in his attempts to drown in his own guilt? "Neither did I," he said, giving her a smile.

"How?" Grace asked.

"Susie made me face up to some home truths," Dean said, raising his eyebrows at her.

"She's a good woman."

"Yes, she is, she's the best," he said. "I need to say sorry to you, Mum."

She frowned at his statement, her hand pulling back.

"I've spent years feeling guilty about the accident, and holding myself responsible for Louisa Smithson's death," Dean said, unable to meet her gaze.

"That wasn't your fault," Grace cut in before he could continue.

"I'm still trying to believe that," he said. "I felt I wasn't good enough, that I didn't deserve the life I had and because of that, I let myself believe you felt the same way too."

"I have never felt that way, Dean. I love you," she said, her words a whisper.

"I know, and I love you too, Mum," he said. "I'm sorry. I'm sorry I pulled away from you and the others, I'm sorry I let my own guilt eat away at our relationship, and I hope it's not too late for me to fix that." Dean looked up, finally meeting her gaze, and trying not to let the tears in her eyes add to the guilt he was trying so hard to shake off. "I love you, Mum," he said.

"I love you too, Dean, and I will always be here for you," Grace said, standing and pulling him to his feet so she could give him a hug.

"About time you sorted that out," Agnes's voice interrupted. Swiping at his own tears, Dean pulled her into their hug.

"Love you too, Granny," he said.

"Of course you do, I'm fabulous," she said. "The real question is, what are you going to do about Susie?"

"Well, for starters, I was thinking I'd move back home," Dean said, holding Grace's gaze. "If you'll have me, that is."

"You always have a home here," she said. "We'd be delighted to have you home. I suspect it'll be a short-lived stay, though."

Dean furrowed his brow in question, but the two women who'd raised him simply met each other's gaze and laughed.

CHAPTER FORTY-ONE

Susie dragged the sponge across the block of colour before focusing on the face in front of her. A few more swipes and she was finished. Her first zebra of the day was pretty good, even if she said so herself.

"You know you'll get stuck doing this at every village fete forever more now, don't you?" Maggie said, taking two pounds from the little girl who was squealing with delight at her new face.

"I don't mind," Susie said, straightening her back with a groan. "At least it was nice to do something other than a mermaid." She'd spent half the morning daubing iridescent scales onto little faces and was likely to be dreaming about them if she did many more.

"Well, now you live in the flat over the cricket pavilion, at least you're close enough that you can still get a lie-in on event days."

Susie smiled at Maggie. Dorothy had finally made it to see the counsellor, and after the first session had declared that she was sick of living in the house she'd shared with her estranged husband. Susie had breathed a sigh of relief at the thought of not having to scrape together enough for the enormous mortgage each month, but had still made her mum wait until her next session before taking any steps to sell the place.

The biggest shock hadn't been that Dorothy wanted to go ahead with the move after that session, but that she'd decided she wanted to live alone. She'd secured one of the council-owned bungalows on the edge of the village and was doing really well. Which meant that for the first time in her life, Susie lived alone, and given how fast the house had sold, she didn't have the pressure of finding the mortgage payments each month. Her mum had insisted on splitting the profits from the sale of the house with her, and Susie figured she'd use the money as a deposit on a place of her own one day. For now, though, she was happy without the responsibility, and renting the flat above the cricket pavilion suited her.

"And I get to enjoy sunny evenings watching the cricket," she said.

"Don't give me that," Maggie said with a laugh. "There isn't a chance in hell you actually watch the cricket; you just like the excuse to sit in the sunshine and drink wine."

"True, but you certainly like joining me," Susie added. "What would you like?" she asked, turning to the little boy who'd appeared in their tent, saving her from whatever reply Maggie was cooking up.

"I want to be a mermaid," he said, grinning at her with a mouth missing half its teeth.

"Okay. What colours would you like?" she asked, pointing to the palette of iridescent paint blocks.

"Here." Susie looked up at the sound of Tess's voice. "I thought you'd need some refreshments."

Susie grinned. "You know me so well," she said, her arm darting out to take the single red velvet cake from the baker before Maggie could get near it.

"This one's for you," Tess said with a smile, producing a second one from behind her back and holding it out to Maggie.

"You definitely know me too well," Susie said, laughing. She started applying the colours the boy had selected to his face.

"I still can't believe you talked Sam Harrison into donating a piece of work to the auction later," Tess said.

"He's the sort of person that always wants to help out. I just can't believe I was stupid enough to put one of my own pieces in as well," Susie said, rolling her eyes. The idea of her own piece going up in an auction near Sam's work was mortifying. It was fine in London where no one knew her, but not here, where everyone knew her, and would remember forever more if it didn't sell, or worse, got a pity bid. "Oh well," she said with a sigh. "Too late to change my mind now."

Standing at the very back of the green, Susie tried to keep her focus off the elevated platform at the front of the gathered crowd. The sun had almost set and was providing a hazy halo-like glow around the trees that ran the length of the field. The committee had run twinkling fairy lights around the sides of the pavilion and down the sides of the field. Combined with the flickering of the tea light candles that were spread out on the bench tables, it gave the whole place a sense of something magical.

"Here," Nathan said, passing Susie and Maggie their drinks.

"Thanks," Susie said, taking a big gulp of the vodka and coke. "I definitely need this."

"It'll work out," Nathan said, giving her a grin that made her wonder just what he was talking about.

She turned to Maggie, who just shrugged and rolled her eyes; clearly she wasn't any the wiser either.

They watched the auctioneer, who was actually the headteacher of the primary school they had all attended. The crowd got quite excited at the chance for a week in the Italian house that the head of the PFTA had purchased a few years before. Bidding went up so high that Susie wondered if the bidders realised they were paying far more than a week's accommodation would normally cost.

"They just want the chance to nosy through her house," Maggie said with a laugh when Susie made her observation out loud.

Some of the lots were less popular; a pedicure by the local beautician went for a fiver, but the woman seemed pleased enough that someone had bid on it.

When it was finally time for her painting to go up for bids, Susie found herself holding her breath. She knew it shouldn't matter if anyone bought it, or what they paid, except for the fact she wanted to help the PFTA raise funds for the new playground, but she found she cared deeply about how the people who'd spent the last few years judging her for her dad's actions responded to her work.

Forcing herself to try to look relaxed, she took a sip of her drink, glad that Maggie squeezed her hand to ground her before her thoughts could spiral.

"Next, we have a painting created by our very own Susie Lucas. If you didn't already know, Susie's work was recently featured in a show by prominent artist Sam Harrison, and all of her work sold on the first night."

Susie felt herself still at the description her old headteacher had given of her. If it wasn't her that was being spoken about, she was sure she'd have been impressed. The fact it was the woman who'd given her a telling-off more than once growing up made it an even more surreal experience.

The chatter around her seemed to grow, her cheeks warming as everyone's heads spun around to look at her. Smiling weakly, she took refuge behind her glass, taking another sip. She was used to people looking at her with mistrust, as though waiting for her to follow in her father's footsteps, but this appraising assessment was something else entirely.

"When this lot is revealed, I think you will all agree that it is an extraordinary piece, and this is a great opportunity to secure a piece of work by an artist who will only go on to achieve huge success, before you have to pay the sort of prices her work will surely attract."

Susie stilled, swallowing as her work was lifted onto the stage and the fabric covering was removed.

As the image was revealed, a hush seemed to pass over the crowd before the chattering restarted even more zealously. A little part of her tension eased at the realisation people liked it. When the bidding began and quickly reached three figures, her relief was complete. These were not pity bids; people genuinely wanted her work.

Letting out a sigh as the bidding slowed down, Susie allowed herself a small smile. She didn't know what sort of bids Sam's work would secure; given that he was a household name, it should certainly be a lot more than hers did, but at least hers had raised a good amount of money, and was going to go for the kind of sum she hadn't dared dream it would get anywhere, never mind at a village fundraising event.

Just as the auctioneer was about to announce the item sold, a voice to the left shouted out a bid double that of the one it was about to go for.

Spinning her head towards the voice, Susie's heart stilled; she knew that voice, but she couldn't let herself believe it was him. Shading her eyes to try to make out the man behind the voice through the twinkling lights that were casting him into shade, she ignored the hum of conversation that seemed to swell.

"Sold," the auctioneer confirmed, making it impossible for the bidder to back out of their foolish act. "Next, we have a piece of art by the world-renowned Sam Harrison…"

Susie found herself unable to glance back to the stage. Her focus was on the man who was now walking towards her. "You didn't need to do that," she said, when Dean finally reached her side.

"I wanted it," he said. "And it's worth far more than I paid."

Susie glanced around, aware that proceedings had been paused while all eyes were on them.

"I assume you'd prefer we don't have this conversation here?" Dean asked, raising a brow at her.

She nodded.

"For the record," he said. "As long as you'll be good enough to let me talk to you, I don't care who hears what I have to say."

She gave him a half smile, still worried about what he could possibly want to say to her after the way she'd left things between them, but grateful for the fact that he respected her dislike of being talked about; she'd had enough of that to last her years, and his excessive bid on her painting was already going to add to that.

They walked quietly, side by side, until they'd passed the edge of the cricket grounds and found themselves walking the lanes of the village they'd grown up in together, circling around the cricket club.

"Why did you make that bid?" she finally asked.

"I wanted the painting you did for the gallery show in London," he said. "But I didn't want to take your success from you by buying it myself."

Susie frowned at him in question.

"Susie, I know you well enough to know that if I'd bought it, you would always have wondered if I'd done it as some sort of pity gesture. I wanted you to know that whoever bought it did so because they loved it, without any doubt."

She stopped walking and studied her feet before turning to face him. "Thank you," she said. "But you still didn't need to bid like that tonight."

Dean laughed and held up a hand to prevent her from commenting before he spoke. "The second I saw that painting tonight, I knew I had to have it."

"Why?" she asked, not really sure she wanted to know the answer, but knowing she'd drive herself mad if she didn't ask.

"I loved your painting for the gallery," he said. "When I looked at it, I could see all my mistakes being peeled back to reveal how things should have been, how they could be, if only I was brave enough."

Susie nodded, surprised that he'd been able to articulate exactly what she'd felt when she'd been creating that work.

"The work I bought tonight was even more powerful; it seemed to scream out at me that redemption was possible." Dean rubbed his hand over his head.

She swallowed; she'd poured her soul into that work, all of the confusion she'd felt over the last few years falling away in the realisation that when people held themselves accountable for their own lives, they could be redeemed.

"Is it?" he asked.

Susie looked up at him with a frown.

"Is redemption possible?" Dean asked, reaching out to lace his fingers through hers.

She studied their entwined hands before forcing herself to look up and meet his eyes. The intensity that greeted her there made her suck in a breath. "Only you can answer that," she finally said, holding his gaze.

"I think it is," he said, giving her a gentle smile, before turning and lifting something from his pocket.

At the sound of a beep and a flash of orange light, Susie realised they'd walked right round to the car park and that Dean had opened a car. It wasn't a sports car, but a solid hatchback that was new enough to be reliable.

"You drove here?" she asked, turning back to him, a smile spreading across her face, before walking over to his car, trying to pull her thoughts together as she ran her hand along the roof.

"I did. I've worked with a driving instructor who specialises in nervous drivers," he said, returning her smile. "I wanted to thank you."

Susie gave him another questioning look.

"I have spent a long time running away from what happened, what I did," Dean said.

"It wasn't..." she began before he interrupted.

"My fault," he said. "I'm not sure I believe that as much as you do, but I'm trying."

She studied him, pleased that he was getting to a better place.

"I have you to thank for putting me on the journey to forgiving myself," he said.

"I didn't do anything," she said.

"You did everything," he replied, reaching forward to take her other hand in his. "I have one more thing to ask of you, though," he said, giving her a nervous smile.

"What?"

"Do you think if we want something enough, wishes can make that dream come true?"

"What?" she said again, aware she was repeating herself but struggling to make sense of his words.

"Well, I realise that I have to be responsible for my own life, and take action to keep making the changes I need, but I was hoping you'd want to be a part of my life again."

Susie's heart sank; she was thrilled that Dean had made the changes he needed to find comfort with himself again, but being relegated to friend was going to hurt, maybe not as much as when he'd just vanished, but enough. "You know I'll always be your friend," she said, dropping her eyes.

Dean took half a step closer, so his chest filled her entire vision. "I'll be grateful to have you back in my life in any way you're prepared to let me," Dean said, his voice coming out broken. "If all you want to be is my friend, I'll be glad to be your friend. But I was hoping you'd be so much more."

Susie glanced up, blinking hard.

"I have dreamed of being with you since I was fifteen, and I hope that if I wish hard enough, and do the work, that dream could come true. I love you, Susie Lucas. I've always loved you."

She stared at him, trying to understand the words he was saying, trying to work out how serious he was. "I don't know if it's enough, Dean," she said with a sigh. "My life is here. Mum's doing so much better, but I still can't leave her."

"Lucky that I quit my job, then," he said, giving her a grin, one hand releasing hers and rising to cup her cheek.

"You quit?" she asked, aware she didn't need to ask him to repeat himself, but trying to absorb his statement, before realisation struck. "You didn't get the partnership, then?"

"I did," he said with a shrug. "I was sitting in a room with Elizabeth and Dipesh, and they were talking away, about to share the decision, which was when I realised I didn't care. When I told them I wanted to resign, they told me they were planning to give me the partnership."

"Wow," she said, trying to work out what that meant; was he taking the promotion or not?

"You were right," he said. "I hated that job; being a partner wasn't going to change that. So, full disclosure, if you agree to being with me, you should know I'm unemployed, and likely to spend the next year working on a project that won't earn me much, if anything."

"You're going to develop that programme that connects people to the support they need?" she asked, and he nodded.

"So, you're offering me the chance to be with a man who has worked through his own issues, and decided on a career path that'll make him happy rather than rich?" she asked, holding his gaze.

Dean gave another nod, his eyes dropping.

"You've forgotten the most important thing," Susie said, her own smile growing.

His head snapped up at her words, a deep frown on his face.

"I love you," she said, leaning forward, her head tilted up towards his. She gently pressed her lips to his.

"Is that a yes, then?" he asked.

Susie nodded, before deepening the kiss.

As Dean backed her into the side of his car, a mewling sound came from behind her.

Pulling away, she swung her head around to find a small bundle of black fur in a pet carrier, the familiar tiny features peering up at her and meowing loudly. "You brought Liquorice?" Susie asked, turning back to Dean.

"She's part of our family," he said with a shrug.

At his words, Susie hauled him back against her and pressed her lips to his.

"It looks like all our wishing really did make our dreams come true," Dean whispered against her mouth.

Without breaking contact, she smiled. "No, facing the truth and working for the things that matter made our dreams come true," she said, wrapping her arms around his neck.

"I'm still going to screw up sometimes," Dean said, pulling her body against his. "But if I promise to keep working on it, will you kiss me again?"

"Always," Susie said, a little piece of her heart shifting back into place at knowing they'd face the challenges to come together.

A NOTE TO THE READER

Dear Reader,

Thank you so much for reading *A Summer of Dreams*. If you have also read *An Imperfect Christmas*, I hope you enjoyed revisiting Honeyford as much as I did. I love writing about this little corner of Somerset and the wonderful people there so I hope you will join us next time as well!

I love visiting London and have been known to spend hours just walking around and simply absorbing everything. It was great being able to bring a little bit of the magic of the city into this story of second chances and being brave enough to try for the life you really want.

Reviews by readers are incredibly important to authors' success these days, so if you enjoyed the novel and would consider taking the time to leave a review, your efforts would be hugely appreciated. Reviews can be left in many places, but you can access **Amazon** and **Goodreads** here.

I love hearing from readers, and would be delighted if you connected with me through my **Facebook page** via **Twitter** or through my **website.**

Here's to escaping into the pages of more heart-warming lives, and loves, together.

Tanya Jean

www.tanyajeanrussell.com

Sapere Books is an exciting new publisher of brilliant fiction and popular history.

To find out more about our latest releases and our monthly bargain books visit our website:
saperebooks.com